A Marshland of His Own

Gavin Zastrow

Orange Hat Publishing
www.orangehatpublishing.com - Waukesha, WI

For information, please contact:

Orange Hat Publishing
www.orangehatpublishing.com
603 N Grand Ave, Waukesha, WI 53186

Edited by Lauren Lisak
Cover design by Brigid Malloy
Chapter heading image by Joe Krause

www.orangehatpublishing.com

The following book is dedicated to my friend Chad Andrew Marsh. As close a friend to me as any that I have ever had, and yet as distant as any of my friends. You will forever be missed and always remembered and loved.

Table of Contents

Introduction

Time heals all wounds . . . . or at least that's what they say . . .

I closed *A Marshland of His Own* one more time. This was the first time I had read it in ten years. Has it really been that long? Wiping a few tears away here and there, the thoughts that ran through my mind in the last four hours all came rushing back. Such a violent combination of pain, sadness, fear, doubt, awakening, personal awareness, healing, suffering. The list just continued on.

While I was at my publisher's office, I was told that I needed to write an introduction to the book to cue my readers into the events of the story, why it was written, and the uniqueness of my point of view as a high school student at that time. I guess that was the real reason I had started reading it again. I wanted the book to be complete and this portion of my life to finally be solidified. The story would be in print, that way I wouldn't have to worry about it getting lost over time.

However, as I got going, I realized that the reason I was re-

reading with such precision was because it was a familiar story that I couldn't quite place. I was lost in my own creation. Twenty-five years is a long time. You meet people. People go their own ways. Thoughts and aspirations you have are replaced by other thoughts and aspirations. The world changes. Your world changes. You change! I have changed a lot over the past two and a half decades and have lost track of the person that wrote this book. It is a perspective I no longer have and no longer could write from, even if I felt inspired to do so. That is one reason it is so special to me.

I can say that the high school me was much like any "normal" high school kid. I wanted to play sports. I wanted to do well in school. I wanted girls to like me. I wanted to be popular. I wanted to fit it, no matter what. I wanted to be happy. I wanted to be successful. I wanted to get into a good college. I thought my world was everyone's world and was really myopic in my own thinking.

As I sat on my porch today, I thought to myself how quickly the twenty-five years have passed. The rain continued to batter the pavement. Every ten seconds or so, I would hear the water displaced on the road as cars passed by. I thought back to earlier in the day and the questions that the publisher asked about me and my story.

Who was the high school you?
Why did you write this?
What was your motivation?
Do you still stay in touch with family?
Do you still stay in touch with the people in this book?
Your parents sound like great people, tell us about them . . .
What about this teacher?
How did you connect with her?

Do you stay in touch with her?

How were you able to be strong enough to write?

Your readers need to know where that voice comes from and where it is now . . .

You know if we publish this, we will have to contact these people . . .

I wasn't prepared for any of that when I entered the office. I simply wanted to put closure on something I did twenty-five years ago, but after reading the story again, I realized it wasn't going to be that simple.

The reason I wrote this story at the time of Chad's suicide was because there was nobody out there who could understand me or my friends. In my mind, we were the first to experience such a heinous event, and it needed to be shared. I felt like no one really cared how we felt or what we were going through, even if they really did. This story was also a result of me feeling like I didn't belong. Chad's suicide was my first real experience with the death of someone close, and I didn't know how to react, how to act, how to cry, how to console, how to grieve. It was the first event in my life that really made me search for who I was, what I was about, what I believed, and what I thought.

I was young enough that I thought there was a right way to do everything in life and that there was one specific way I was supposed to handle this. My world was so confined and I only looked at it from my short-sighted point of view. I didn't realize that that wasn't the case and that things get messy all the time in life. There are so many points of view, there are so many perspectives, and they all make sense in their own way. Life can get really complicated.

As a young kid, I couldn't see that because I didn't share my perspective, people didn't understand it. I didn't understand that people actually didn't know how I felt because they had never been close with anyone that had killed themselves. All people have first-time experiences with death. Some are as painful as what my group of friends faced. Some are different because of where people are in life, their experiences, their beliefs, their support systems.

As a result of reading *A Marshland of His Own* this afternoon, I realized that for some of the questions that I was asked by the publisher, I had just forgotten the answers. However, I also realized something surprising happened as well. I found there were parts of the book that I no longer remember and for some, I wondered why I even included them. In looking at my notes, I vaguely remember starting the project as a short story just to get the emotions out and being encouraged by a cousin that I had to keep going with it. A teacher helped me edit and develop it, but I don't remember how or when we met or accomplished the edits since I never had her as a teacher and this was long before the days of email.

As a result, I am inspired by my high school self to show the world the point of view that I myself can not fully understand anymore. Every year I get further away from this event, I am further away from that version of myself and that understanding of myself. *A Marshland of His Own* allows me to journey back to that perspective and remember events with an order and specificity that I would not be able to remember today or even be able to put to paper.

Ultimately, I believe this was one of the reasons I wrote this story down and why I struggled through those feelings my senior year. I have had some events in my life that have forced similar "raw emotions," but the reason I am able to slip so vividly back to this one is because I went through the hard work of documenting the pain that I experienced at that time in my life. The voice is so loud that I don't believe most readers can ignore it even if they haven't had a similar experience. I remember feeling like I was making myself go through the pain a second time as I wrote it, but I never shared that with anyone because I didn't want them to make me stop writing.

As an adult reading this book, I am also aware that many kids struggle with many of the same questions I once faced, even if they aren't dealing with a suicide of a friend. The general questions, images, and emotions are relatable to many modern day problems of gun violence, opioid deaths, etc. But most people don't get to see inside the mind of a "normal" teenager to see what they are thinking, why they are thinking that way, and how they are processing it.

Ultimately, I believe that I didn't know what to do with the mixed array of emotions I had at this point in my life. I believe I wrote in an attempt to heal, and as I started to heal, I was inspired by my parents, family, teachers, and friends to continue writing because they saw the value of the viewpoint. Looking back, I truly believe this process allowed me to heal and move on instead of becoming messed up and destroying my own life as I mention frequently in the story.

Time heals all wounds . . . or at least that's what they say . . . I'll let you decide.

Part 1: Mourning

The Reality of Life and Death

Reality has come, Reality has gone
Life is so short and yet so long
A friend has passed. He is set to rest
for eternity. What makes this best?
I do not understand the meaning of this
It's so unfair. He will be missed.
An explanation or note would have been nice
but nothing is there for my feelings to entice
I must go on living my life the way I
always have, holding onto the memories that
pierce me like knives I will struggle with them
and carry their weight even though they bring me
HATE

The Explosive Beginning and Ending

It was a cool, fall Sunday morning in the middle of October, the day after our school's homecoming dance. Many of us were sleeping late into the morning to catch up on the sleep that we had lost during the weekend. We wouldn't realize until later that day the tragedy that had occurred while we were sleeping.

BANG!

That sound would be all that the students of that small town would hear for the rest of the week. It would stay with them forever and never be forgotten. It would linger through the town as the horizon seems to linger on forever. The lifeline of that small town had received a major wound that would be irreparable. It had lost a vein of life through the act of a mysterious bullet. Mysterious in the fact that, to other towns, it was just another terrible and unfortunate incident, but somehow as you looked around our town, this incident was not just another statistic. This was the loss of an individual, a loss that would change the essence and the spirit of that town. It would grow and unite in the upcoming weeks. Mysterious in the fact that it would change the rest of the lives of those that were close to the victim in ways that were unfathomable. We, the high school students, had just taken one of the most important classes of our lives and learned a lesson that none of us would forget, no matter where we were in life. Life is not a game, and it is as fragile as any piece of glass. Mysterious in the fact that it was a sudden and unexpected event that would leave many emotionally scarred for the rest of their natural lives. Chad Marsh, a friend of mine, had destroyed his life and drastically affected every one of us who had ever known him.

He shot himself in the head.

He was only sixteen.

He somehow must have felt that life was no longer worth living and that it would be easier just to end it instead of facing his problems, whatever they may have been. At least that's all I can guess because he left no explanation. There was no note. Nothing. All that I was left with were my feelings and a whole lot of pain, and all I could say was "Why?" I had feelings that I had never experienced, and I didn't know what to do with them.

I felt angry because Chad committed such a horrible and stupid act.

I felt guilty because I couldn't help thinking that there was something that I could have said to him to stop him from doing this horrendous deed.

I felt depressed because this close friend didn't understand how many close friends he truly had.

I felt sad for the loss of my friend.

I felt afraid of what the future would hold for me and my friends.

I felt disgusted at the act of suicide.

These feelings were rotating in a never-ending cycle of confusion in my mind.

I was filled with memories of him and the way he lived his life. He was someone who always dared to run on the edge, but on this day, the edge crumbled and a landslide of pain was created from this loose soil that sent our small town into mourning and Chad into a marshland of his own. He sent the members of my town on a trip in which they would explore the reality of life and death. We would learn together that although they are two entirely different things, they are similar in many ways. Life, as well as death, is scary, difficult to understand, a place for new beginnings, and a place for so many things that will never cease to fascinate and frighten the people of the world. Ironically, because of the unfortunate doing of a sixteen-year-old, we were going to achieve an immediate understanding of the unknown. It was amazing.

Even through his death, Chad was going to continue his uncanny ability of spreading knowledge to those of us who knew him. He had always seemed to have an ability to find the right answer, but now, it was as if Chad didn't have the knowledge and had chosen the wrong answer. He left behind a marshland that was full of pain and suffering. This marshland could have been the pain that none of us knew that he felt. Or it could have been the pain that the small community encountered due to his death. Chad left one marshland where things are often unpredictable only to go to another marshland of uncertainty and the unknown.

Bloody Sunday

It was that bloody Sunday morning. I woke up at eleven o'clock after staying overnight at a friend's house. The memories of this day are vivid to me for one simple reason: my parents. I arrived home around eleven-thirty that morning and was immediately hounded by my parents with questions. How was the dance? Did you have fun? It went on and on, almost as if they had stayed up all night preparing a list of questions with which to annoy me when I got home. It was the type of situation that you hate, but on the other hand you love. It continued for a long time, or at least it seemed that way. This only ended when my brother woke up. He too had gone to the dance the evening before, and it was now his turn to be interrogated by our parents. They stopped grilling me for details and attempted to squeeze some out of him.

I was finally free to go take a shower and change into a fresh set of clothes. I had to laugh to myself over how enthusiastic my parents had been. It was something that, however annoying it may have been, for some reason continued the good mood I was feeling. I recalled the things I had told them and the things I hadn't. The weekend had been so much fun. It was as much fun as the weekend that I had a couple of weeks earlier.

A group of my friends had gathered to go pumpkin smashing. Pumpkin smashing was a Halloween activity that was well participated in by high school students. We would meet at someone's house and run through the neighborhoods, smashing the pumpkins that were lying around in yards and on doorsteps. It was crazy. The citizens of the community hated it, but it was fun because it was silly and stupid, which was also the whole reason for being involved – getting chased by owners of homes as well as police.

I especially remember this mission of pumpkin smashing due to a pumpkin I saw Chad smash. It appeared to be perfectly round and seemed to have no flaws. It was bright orange and had been carved with triangular eyes and rigid, jagged teeth. It was so beautiful, and it was almost a shame that we had to smash it. However, when Chad picked it up, the middle was all rotted. He smashed it in the middle of the street. Then we noticed all these bugs on the pavement that we had been unable to see before. They were crawling around on the street as if they had finally escaped the pumpkin.

We walked over to examine the pumpkin a little closer and noticed that the bugs had been eating away at the inside of the pumpkin as if they were hoping to find the outside. I was about ready to pick a piece of the pumpkin up when we saw the owner of the house open his door. He was angry and running at us with a baseball bat. He said that he had called the cops, and we could hear the sirens on their way. The man was huge. He wore a t-shirt and a pair of blue pants, and his gut rumbled at us. We all knew that it was time to run quickly to a house where we knew we would be safe.

We took off and outran the man easily because of his immense size. We had also left quickly enough that the police would have no chance to find us. That night was filled with events like that, events of adolescent invincibility.

I grinned as I stepped out of the shower and thought of the fact that even though I didn't have the greatest time at the dance, it didn't matter because my friends and I were together. I was now primed to finish the memorable weekend by watching the Packers play on TV. I stopped and looked out the window at the perfect fall day. The weather was calm and peaceful, the sky was blue, and there was a light breeze.

It was time to sit down and watch the game as I did every weekend with my brother and my dad. We would often bet on the games: who would win, who would lose. It was almost a tradition of sorts. The ball was kicked off from the Buccaneers to the Packers. That is all I remember about the game itself. I believe the Packers won, but it must not have been much of a game because it was a rarity that I would not watch a whole Packer game.

However, on this Sunday, I stopped watching the game, probably because my one brother had gone to his girlfriend's house, my dad had gone to watch the game with my mom and little brother, who had been watching on another television, and I had to read a book for English class. It was supposed to be read by Monday, and, of course, I had let it go to the point where I had to read the entire book today. Still, I felt I could do it. I felt like I could do anything on this weekend. I felt invincible. All until I received that phone call. Then the feeling of invincibility became an illusion.

I was around page seventy-eight in The Catcher in the Rye when the phone rang. It was my friend's dad attempting to locate his son. He had a different tone in his voice that was so much more serious and scared than usual. He asked me if I knew where he could find his son. I told him that I didn't know where he was, but if I heard from him, I'd let him know that he should call home.

Then he gave me some of the worst news of my life. He said to me, "So, I guess you heard the bad news by now."

I said, "No. Why, what's wrong?"

And that was how I found out. He told me that Chad's body had been discovered. He had committed suicide.

"What?"

He repeated his words.

I asked how. I asked when. I asked where.

He responded, "I have no details." And said good-bye.

I was shocked. I began to make myself believe that I had heard him wrong. I went back to the TV, and I vaguely heard my parents ask me who was on the phone. I repeated the conversation back to them, word for word. Their faces lost all expression. I could tell that they were also shocked, but it seemed as if I was more shocked than them. They opened their arms to comfort me and tell me that it would be alright. "This is the second time in two weeks that you have told us such unbelievable news." That was because a couple weeks earlier, I had come home with the news that my friend's dad had died of a heart attack. He had only been in his forties. It seemed too young to die, and now Chad, who was all of sixteen, was gone.

I went over to the big picture window in our living room and stared at the lake next to where we lived. It was so alive. There were waves moving along, fish occasionally jumping, and the sun shining off the water in a friendly way. This angered me. This had been such a beautiful fall day, but now it had turned into one of confusion, pain, anger, disgust, sadness, and depression. I must have been staring out the window and thinking for almost twenty minutes. Actually, I don't even think I can say that I was thinking because I wasn't. I felt like I had the life ripped out from inside of me.

I decided to take a walk through the streets of my neighborhood, but this only increased the feelings of confusion that I had. I remember looking at the sky and thinking that it should be black. The breeze that was serene before was now blowing me over. I felt as if I was carrying a ten-ton suitcase of pain and disgust. Chad's death was the worst pain that I had ever faced in my entire life. It was so hard to deal with, something that no man, woman, or child should ever have to deal with for as long as they live. I was alone with my thoughts. "This could not have happened. There was no way that one of my friends could kill himself."

I began to ask myself questions that were impossible to answer. "What happens to people when they die? What happens to people who create their own deaths? Do they go to heaven or hell?" I was left with only what had been taught to me when I went to a Lutheran grade school, but it was difficult to recall knowledge from so long ago. I stopped walking and looked into the sky, praying that Chad would not be punished eternally for his terrible mistake. I felt the need to talk to someone. I lived a ways out of town, so I decided to go talk to my neighbor. I went over to his house and discovered that he was pledging a fraternity. We hardly even talked about my problem, mainly because I barely mentioned it and didn't want to talk about it in the hollow hope that it would go away. I did release some of the frustration I had just by participating in a conversation. He was talking about how difficult it was to pledge a fraternity and that it was a lot of hard work, but I didn't really care about what he was saying. I just wanted to avoid being alone.

Then it hit me. I was growing up, and the ladder of life was beginning to confront me with steeper steps and bigger problems. In order to truly learn the answers to my questions, I had to learn my feelings about life and death. I had to stop listening to everyone else's beliefs and decide what I believed. If I didn't come to some conclusions, I would always be left with the questions I had, and I would never be able to deal with the feelings of confusion, anger, sadness, and sickness I had from the day's events.

I went home and decided to hide from my feelings. I would not let my family see how much this event was affecting me, so I went home and buried myself in my homework. I read for almost an hour but only covered ten pages. Out of those ten pages, I remembered nothing. It was scary. I was lost. It was then that I received a phone call from one of my friends telling me that a bunch of my classmates were going to meet and discuss their feelings regarding Chad's suicide. I jumped at the opportunity because it seemed to be a way to get rid of the lonely feeling I had and a chance to express my feelings of pain.

I rushed through the house at a frantic pace, looking for my car keys. Suddenly, I heard a voice from behind, demanding to know what I was doing. I looked up and saw my mom.

"What are you doing?" she repeated.

I responded, "I'm looking for my car keys. Have you seen them?"

"Yeah, they're on the mantel. Your dad put them there so that you wouldn't lose them."

"He's always moving things. Doesn't he know that when he organizes things, I lose them?"

My mom continued to look at me. "Where are you going?"

"I'm going over to a friend's house. He just invited me over. He said a whole lot of my friends were going to be at his house, and we're going to talk about Chad. I guess the news really was true."

She paused for a few seconds. "Okay. What time are you going to be home? Remember, it's a school night."

"I don't know. Whenever it breaks up, I guess. I hadn't really thought about it."

"Okay. I hope it helps. Just remember, you have school tomorrow."

"I know. I know," I mumbled as I started out the door.

My mom yelled, "Wait! There isn't going to be any alcohol, is there?"

I looked at her, then said, "Of course not. I can't believe you said that, Mom." I stepped out the door, thinking to myself, "I wonder if there is going to be any? I can't believe she automatically thought that. Doesn't she trust me? I can't believe she thinks that I would go party at a time like this. Sure, I drink, just like everyone else, but to accuse me of going to get drunk? Not tonight. I can't believe she said that. I know she knows I party, but . . ." I walked down the sidewalk and climbed into my car.

The House of Healing

I drove over to where my friends were going to gather. It was hard for me to keep my feelings within me so I could drive. I'll never forget hearing a song on the radio that night. The song was "It's So Hard to Say Goodbye To Yesterday" by Boyz II Men. I thought to myself how it was kind of ironic that such a song would come on the radio at this exact moment. It made my stomach churn and the feelings inside of me kept moving around. I turned it off because it held too much pain. Chad's deathly act was hard on me, but it was also very difficult for anyone else who had ever known him.

I arrived at my friend's house, still denying that there was any truth to this whole situation. It seemed like one horrendous, terrifying dream from which I could not escape.

I'll never forget walking into that house and seeing all my friends huddled in that tiny room, staring at the TV with blank white looks on their faces. It was as if a ghost had just flown through the room. I walked in and heard the sound of the TV muffled by that of young adults crying. "Parker Lewis Can't Lose" was on. It was weird because even though it was difficult hearing the TV over all the crying, I heard the final line of the show: "We sometimes don't appreciate our friends enough until they are gone." This quote went through me like a stake through my heart. It was exactly how I felt. I hadn't ever appreciated my friendship with Chad as much as I did at that moment. That line sparked the group to expose some of their feelings and get them out into the open, but I, for the most part, just sat and listened. It was so hard for me to release the feelings I had. I don't know if I was afraid to or if it was just because I had never had such strong feelings in my life, but I slowly let some of them out.

The group did what needed to be done, and I sat there and gave support. Support was what was needed, not by parents, but by people who were experiencing the tragedy firsthand. They were better able to understand how I was feeling.

The group was an interesting array of students. On this night, there were no cliques. We were all in the same sinking boat, and it didn't matter whether you were a jock or a dirt-ball, a good student or a bad student. All that mattered was that we were there for each other. We shared stories about Chad, both the good times and the bad, that made us laugh and feel a little better inside.

I'll never forget talking with a teacher that we invited that evening. Although I never had her as a teacher, I felt comfortable talking to her. She was the type of lady who made you feel special no matter who you were or if she knew you or not. She told me that we had to remember Chad for what he was, and that we should live our lives the way we always did, holding on to those memories.

At the time, I didn't understand what she meant. It was just another piece of advice that would confuse me more. I remember thinking to myself, "You can't understand what I'm feeling. It wasn't one of your best friends that died. It was just one of your students." But, it still seemed like good advice, so I decided to try and follow it.

Now I understand that I will be following it for the rest of my life.

As the night developed, I remember everyone appearing to feel a little better, except me. The feeling of loneliness was growing inside of me again. I would hear kids beginning to laugh, and I couldn't help but think, "How can you laugh so soon, so easily after such a horribly terrifying and painful incident?" It was difficult for me to accept any reason that would justify happiness. The night wore on, and people began to go to sleep. I didn't sleep; I didn't even try. Instead, I drank endless amounts of coffee and soda to stay awake. At the time, I thought that it was the grimy taste of the coffee and the soda that kept me awake and kept me going, but now I realize that I was just plain afraid to go to sleep. I was afraid that I might see Chad in my dreams, or worse yet, that he wouldn't be there at all. I was afraid that I might never wake up.

Mysterious Monday

The next day, the sun rose, and it kind of surprised me. Yesterday, when I first heard the news, I had this feeling that the sun would never rise again. My mom had told me that the world would keep on going, and that it was just a difficult event I had to deal with, yet inside of me, the world had stopped. Time was frozen, and I felt bitter cold. I watched the sun rise on this morning, and it was such a beautiful sight. The sky had this magnificent line of red which was just above a sparkling line of orange. Above all of that was powder blue. It was amazing how the sun seemed to appear out of the horizon, almost out of nowhere, passing through each of the settings in the sky. The world had continued to live, with or without Chad.

This was my first time watching a sunrise, and I've seen many since, but none have been so beautiful. It is probably because on this particular occasion, I was alone. There was no one there to ruin it or make it better. As the sun cast its beauty on another day, I was filled with mixed emotions. It was a new day with new faces. New life could begin at any moment, but I was now faced with the terrifying reality that life could also end at any moment.

Slowly, each one of my friends arose from where they had been sleeping and got ready to head off to school. It was incredible how quiet they were. I had the impression that their silence was due to more than their tiredness. I knew many of them were still attempting to deal with their feelings.

The house cleared out rather quickly, but it was still early, so a few of my friends and I went to McDonald's before heading to school. The smell of the morning food almost made me sick. I ordered a coffee and slid into a booth in the middle of the restaurant where I saw the employees frantically working. They smiled and appeared to be having fun while they rushed through their work. I looked at my friends sitting across from me. Their faces lacked any expression, and everyone seemed to be in a daze. The vinyl cushions on the back of the booths were gold and green. I thought to myself, "Why are they so bright?" The lack of conversation gave me an eerie feeling. I started to drink some more coffee to avoid any chance of dozing off in school. I must have had two or three cups before grabbing another one to save for when I got to school.

We left McDonald's and bravely headed for the high school. We knew that today would be rough. People would be constantly asking us for the true story behind Chad's death and if we knew the exact details of the weekend events. It would be difficult. I remember it as the roughest day of high school that I have ever experienced. There was no homework, no teachers, and no assignments. The only thing I did on that Monday was talk with my friends and counselors. When I walked into the school, I had a feeling in my stomach that I could not place. It is one I have never felt again and one I probably will never be able to explain. It was almost a feeling of fear, of exhaustion, or even an overload of coffee. The weird feeling that plagued me also set in stronger as I attempted to set aside all my feelings about Chad's death. I walked through the hallways and saw all these students, but I didn't hear a sound, almost as if I was watching a TV with no volume.

It was unusual for me to be at school so early. I normally would arrive about five minutes after school actually started and race down the empty halls to study hall, tardy. On this day, the halls were packed. I went to my locker and got the materials I needed before heading off to an area of wooden benches, far from my first class, where my friends were sitting. I sat down next to them and began to drink my coffee. It was cold and had lost its taste, and the cardboard left a grungy taste in my mouth. I looked around. No one was saying anything. The first bell rang, and it echoed endlessly through the halls. It seemed to ring constantly in my ears for a couple of minutes.

I regained my composure, gathered my stuff, and headed for study hall. I figured that the only way to deal with the weekend was to go to study hall and bury myself in homework. The second bell rang, and I attempted to read The Catcher in the Rye for English class. It was no use. My mind just could not concentrate.

Then, my study hall teacher asked the students to give him their attention. He was nearing retirement and had been one of my most favorite teachers throughout high school. He was the kind of teacher who cared for the students first and worried about grades after he was sure the student learned the material. When I came into class late almost every day, he would let me come in without giving me a detention. He did, however, always make me give him an excuse. It was always a challenge for me to come up with a new one every day that he hadn't heard before.

My teacher stood up and said that he had an announcement he was supposed to make. I put my head down because I knew what was coming. He then read a letter from the principal that had been issued to every class in the school which bluntly explained to the entire school body that over the weekend, a student at our high school, Chad Marsh, had taken his life by way of a gun. After he read the announcement, my teacher said that we could resume work. I lifted my head and looked across the study hall. Two of my friends broke into tears and left the room. The pain had once again broken through. The announcement also affected me, but for some reason, no tears came. I became scared. The multitude of feelings were back again. I attempted to do homework for another five minutes before I realized that there was no way I would ever be able to concentrate.

I left study hall and wandered through the halls, continually asking myself one little question. "Why?" After ten minutes or so, I went to the Little Theater, which was where we were supposed to go if we needed to get away from class. It was here that the school had brought in outsiders to help us deal with the emotional highs and lows of the weekend. There were priests, ministers, psychologists, social workers, and some others that were unknown to me. We needed them all, if not more. Many of us as individuals had gone from one of the highest points in our lives to one of the lowest, all in a couple of days.

I walked in and saw all my friends crying and in terrible pain and each of the counselors attempting to help. I sat down, and even though I knew I belonged, I felt out of place. Everyone was in touch with how they felt, but I was just there. I thought to myself, "What's wrong with me? Why can't I let my feelings out the way everyone else is?" Then the fifty-two minute class period was over, so I grabbed my books, my courage, and headed for my second hour class.

It was in my second hour class that I experienced one of my most vivid and painful memories. As I walked in, I noticed some quotes that were posted in the front of the room, quotes that I had never noticed before. They seemed to be meaningless little catchy phrases, but one quote grabbed my attention and ate away the inside of me. It said, "It is never too late to be what you might have been." This made me sick as I thought of Chad. It truly was too late for him, and he would never be what he might have been.

I wanted to leave the room because the hurt was becoming too great to bear, and I knew there was no way that I would be able to study or learn anything. But the teacher didn't allow me to leave until I got the test back that we had taken on Friday. It had been an important test, one that I needed to get a B on to maintain a B in the class. I got it back with a score of 58%: an F. It didn't matter to me. As I looked at the score, I thought, "It doesn't matter, nothing matters, because sooner or later everything we do will be forgotten or destroyed."

Then a good friend of mine and I got ready to leave the room. She was brilliant and rarely wrong, and she sat next to me, so I would often copy off her paper. Another girl who sat just in front of her decided to join us, and the three of us arose and huddled together. We left class and went to the Little Theater. The rest of the morning seemed to drag on in a blur, moving along in slow motion. The main thing I remember is leaving the Little Theater and standing outside, just staring at the parking lot and thinking, "How could this happen?" This idea had been eating at me and was something that I had no control over. I thought I was alone until a counselor snuck up from behind. He asked me, "What are you thinking?"

Startled, I wanted to respond with all the thoughts circling my head. Instead, I just told him that I needed some fresh air.

"I've been watching you. You came out here more than ten minutes ago. Come on. What's really wrong?" I didn't answer. "It's my job. I'm a counselor. You can open up to me."

With that statement, I responded, "I'm not sure."

"What do you mean?"

"Well, I see all my friends crying and in so much pain, but I can't feel that way. I'm so angry and so sad. I don't understand how Chad could do this. I feel sad, but for some reason I can't allow the tears to flow like everyone else."

"I see. It's a difficult process, but you have to give it time. Eventually, you will come to grips with how you feel." We talked for a while, but it couldn't have made much of a difference because the only thing I remember is going back inside the school.

The bell for lunch rang, and everyone was getting ready to meet at one girl's house. I was friends with her and thought it would be fun to go. Other friends of mine were going too, intent on missing their afternoon classes and their afternoon sports practices. I wanted to do that very thing, pick up and leave, but for some reason I decided to stay. I guess I mainly wanted to stay so that I could go to football practice and try to take my anger out on other players during the drills. The afternoon is still a vague cloud to me. There is little that I want to remember or that I can remember. However, I do remember sitting through half of my history class. It was taught by the football coach and was usually a fun class because he was always cracking jokes and making it interesting. On this day, I don't think I laughed once, and I don't remember having fun at all. Chad's death had clouded my mind and taken over my life.

After school that day, I went to practice, intent on releasing some of my bottled-up emotions. The coaches did not allow us to do any hitting drills that day, but they did let us run plays on the scout team. It was so frustrating and embarrassing. I attempted to hit people as hard as I could, but I would just miss and fall on my face. I must have looked like a complete idiot, but no one said a word. They simply let me work out the pain on my own, and I have always been thankful to them for that. It was an unusual practice because we were missing a lot of guys and then there were a handful of players like me who just could not seem to do anything right. After practice, I traveled home with just as much anger and confusion as I had at the beginning of practice. As a matter of fact, I think I may have had more.

An Evening Experience

It had been a long day, and I was in a state of continual turmoil and shock. I still had not accepted the fact that Chad was dead. I sat at home watching TV, saying to myself, "Chad's just playing a huge, bad joke. He's out there somewhere laughing, and I'll see him again." Those feelings of gut-wrenching pain and that uneasy feeling of an unknown daze were something I had from the moment I heard the news. I had always denied it, and even today I attempted to deny that reality. There are times that I like to imagine that Chad just went on a vacation, and he'll be coming back any day now. These kinds of thoughts just tend to increase the grief that I have felt and are of no help to me in the process of healing. Yet, that doesn't stop me from thinking them.

I made it home from football practice, and my mom told me that if I needed anyone to talk to, she was there for me. I didn't want to talk, but I didn't want to be alone. That confused feeling led me to call one of my friends and see what was going on. I asked him if he was going to Young Life. Young Life was a youth group that gathered once a week and held services. It was different than any other youth group because the whole service was organized and run for the most part by kids. It was something that I had never attended. I had always thought to myself, "It isn't worth going to. Just another little clique that gathers once a week and gossips." I had no idea what went on there or even what the group was about. My friend said he was going and that I should go too. "There are going to be a lot of people there. It should be good for all of us," I remember him saying. I climbed into my car and began to drive over there. On the way, I noticed how beautiful the sky appeared to be. There were millions of stars that seemed to light up the whole town. It was as if they were supplying the town with the energy it needed.

I had the radio on, and for the second time in two days, the song "It's So Hard to Say Goodbye To Yesterday" came on. It was so painful to hear the lyrics. This time, though, I didn't change the station. It was almost as if I needed to hear the song. Even though it hurt to listen, it relaxed me and helped me to come a little bit closer to my true feelings.

I started to think, "If there really is a God, why does he allow such horrible things to occur? It isn't fair." With these thoughts, I momentarily began to lose faith in the idea that there was a God.

I arrived at the student's house where Young Life was being held. I was shocked; I had to park almost a mile down the road because of all the people that were there. It was amazing, and I couldn't help thinking, "Maybe there is something to this group after all." I walked up to the door. Did I belong here?

I reached for the doorbell, and strangely enough, the door opened before I even hit the bell. The people at the door were not the slightest bit surprised that I was there. They simply said, "Welcome. The rest of the group is just about ready to begin downstairs." I walked down the stairs and noticed that the huge basement was packed wall-to-wall with people. Everyone looked so close and united, like we were a family that had just lost one of its members. It was so crowded that there were people sitting all the way up and down the staircase.

I managed to weave my way through the mounds of people in an attempt to sit by my closer friends, and they squeezed together so that I could sit down. The service began, and all my friends immediately grabbed tissues, getting prepared for the tears that were going to come.

In the past, it had always been uncool for me to sing. I never really liked it much either. However, on this night, my friends and I huddled together and sang magnificently. It was another way to release the hurt that we were feeling.

Then, after the service portion concluded, we were told to break off into little groups and just share our feelings with the group. So many different emotions were floating around that room. I remember sitting in my group, not knowing exactly what my feelings were, but I do remember seeing my friends in terrible pain. One of my friends couldn't even share his feelings because he was drowning in his own tears. He was so torn apart.

Then I caught a glimpse of myself in the mirror. I looked so pathetic; I had no tears, and it appeared as if I had no sorrow. The fact that I couldn't cry for the death of a close friend was bad enough, but to see myself look as though it wasn't even affecting me, that scared me. I stopped listening to everyone else's feelings, and my mind began to wander. "I don't deserve to live if I can't even shed a tear for such a good friend. Am I really this cold and this emotionless?" The messages that I had heard from Scripture and the songs that we sang that night helped many to relieve some of the grief that they were experiencing. I, on the other hand, was trapped in a land of confusion, and no one, not even God, could supply the answers I needed to escape. I felt worse instead of feeling better.

The adults that had come to the meeting saw me as someone who had already dealt with the sadness of the situation. They went around and tried to comfort those who were in obvious torment. I sat there wondering, "Is there anyone else in this town that feels like me, so hurt, and yet so out of place?"

The meeting ended, and it was time to leave. I looked around the room and could not help but feel sick to my stomach. I tried to find people who just wanted to hang out all night, but it was no use. I was going to have to go home and face what awaited me in my dreams.

I went home and talked to my mom for a while about life after death. Then she went to bed, and I watched hours and hours of TV. I was trying to hide, but it was no use. I gathered myself and went up to my room.

It was going to be the first time I tried to sleep in almost two days. I felt exhausted, but I wasn't even tired. I lay in bed for what felt like an eternity, asking myself one question: "Why, Chad? Why?" I slowly dozed off into a nightmarish dream, then woke up in an immense sweat, scared as the darkness became an evil possessor that crept throughout my room.

Reflections

Life is an image of reality; Reality is an image of death;
Death is the only one image of life.

The young man lay in his bed, staring into the darkness. He was only able to see the black sky outside his window. He rolled over and attempted to rest his weary eyes once again. It was no use. The battle inside his mind was too much. The image he had just seen in his dream was too powerful. The world no longer appeared real; it was an image containing all too much heartache. The young man thought to himself, "Maybe if I get up and get a drink of water, I'll feel better. Anything is worth a try." He pushed his body out of bed.

He rose and stumbled, attempting to reach the light switch in his room. He turned it on, the artificial light creating a strange effect. It felt like real sunlight, but it also felt fake. This was another realistic vision in which he noticed that everything around him was fake. There was nothing that was real, including life. The young man decided to clean up his room and do anything else that was possible in order to avoid the dreams that awaited him. He was afraid to face reality; he was terrified to face the world beyond reality.

He decided that he needed a little soothing music to calm his nerves. The young man started shaking furiously as he heard the music. He was listening to a country song, and the lyrics talked about having friends in low places. "What happened to my friend?" he wondered. "Life isn't fair." He backed towards his bed but suddenly stopped in his tracks as he crossed by a mirror. The reflection of his image frightened him. He saw a lonely, confused teenager who was scared of the world. He stood in front of the mirror for half an hour, picking out physical defects. "Why am I so ugly? I have all these pimples on my face. My hair is the wrong length and color. My eyes are the wrong color. I'm too short. I'm overweight." He was unable to see one good quality in himself. He began to feel better by making himself feel worse.

"It should have been me." This was the thought that continually crossed through his mind. The image he saw of himself did not correspond with the way the world looked at him. Society saw him as a rising young adult, a kid who was very powerful. People saw him as a muscular kid who always appeared to be on top of the world. He was known as someone who was always able to act older than he was. This was especially true now. His friend's suicide had affected all of his friends in noticeable ways. Many looked at him and saw him adjusting. He never cried. It seemed as if he knew how to handle the situation. He was dependable and looked upon as someone who was smart enough to find his own answers.

The young man seemed ready to go to bed now. He was still reluctant, but there was nothing else he could do. As he started to walk away from the mirror, all of a sudden, his reflection changed.

He was still staring at the mirror, but the image the mirror sent back was of a little boy in tears. It was himself, but much younger, when he was in sixth grade. The young blond-haired boy was wearing a red sweater with one row of diamond checkers that went across the front of his chest. He had on a pair of blue jeans and a watch on his left wrist. A small smile was on his face, then, as if being reminded of a date with destiny, he quickly glanced at his watch. He appeared to mouth the words, "It's time," to his image and then began to cry. The young man sat and stared at this boy mouthing words and crying as if something dreadful was about to happen.

Once again, his image changed. The young boy that had momentarily surfaced in the mirror had all but disappeared. Now the image was that of another child. He appeared to be the same, yet for some unexplainable reason, he seemed completely different. This boy was also crying. He was wearing a red flannel shirt with a diamond pattern like that of the earlier image. However, this diamond pattern spread over the entire flannel. There was something unusual about the pattern. The black and red diamonds were obviously different colors, but they seemed to blend into a confusing array of colors. The image was recognizable, but no name could be placed to it. It was something out of the past that had once been clear, but had now been forgotten. The image started to change again.

The red from the checkered pattern appeared to displace itself on the mirror, and a fog materialized as if to cover something up. It quickly disappeared, leaving the young man with a horrifying image. The gruesome picture made him want to cry. A young adult, a friend, lay before him in a pool of blood. His blond hair was contaminated by streaks of red, and his smile, his grin, couldn't be found here. A gun was in the distance . . . a gun that was miles away and, therefore, unidentifiable. The friend, however, seemed as if he could be touched. The young man reached out and poked the mirror with his finger. The image was just that, an image. The rough beard that was beginning to grow was surprisingly noticeable, and it looked as though it was going to fall off his face.

The young man gathered his courage and again attempted to reach out and touch the image. This time he was successful. He felt the roughness of the beard, the reality of the skin, the texture of the blood, and he tried to lift him, but it was no use. Then he screamed in a whimpering voice, "Why? Why? Why? It's not fair!" The image slowly faded away. The young man wanted the image to leave and never come back. It was too agonizing and too realistic. Yet he wanted the image to last forever. It might be the last chance he would ever have to see his friend again. The experience was so tangible and drastic that it had confused and scared him.

The image left, and the young man again saw his own reflection in the mirror. He cried for the image of his friend to reappear, but it never did. He started to shake more furiously than before. His image still scared him because now every time he looked into the mirror, he imagined himself with a hole in his head. He suddenly realized that sleep and the agonizing dreams that it held were always going to find him, whether he was asleep or not. Reality had no bounds, and life is always full of questions without answers, especially simple answers.

Life is an image of reality; Reality is an image of death;
Death is the only one image of life.

The Day of Truth

Each day seemed like an eternity, plagued with the same problems and no answers. Each hour of school felt like a repeat of the one before it. "Why won't the grief come out?" is all I could ask myself. "Why won't the awful pain that I have inside of me get any easier?" It was now Tuesday. It was the day I dreaded since I heard of Chad's death.

It was the day that I was going to be forced to attend a funeral. I was being forced to go by my conscience. I had carried guilt all through my life for not being able to attend the funerals of those who were close to me.

The guilt had become most severe in the weeks preceding Chad's funeral. My uncle had died, and I had felt a need to attend his funeral. I wanted to say goodbye, but I didn't know how. I went to his wake and paid my respects, but when it came time for the actual funeral, I escaped to a place where I felt safe. I went home. I had suppressed all the feelings that were necessary to express, and it was a mistake, but it was something that could not be changed. I did not want to make the same mistake with Chad.

The funeral was going to be my chance to say goodbye to Chad. The entire day I wondered what the purpose of a funeral was. Why were they so "important" and "meaningful"? I thought I had the answer, but I wasn't quite sure. I knew it would be difficult to deal with a funeral, but I figured it couldn't be any more difficult than facing the dreams that I had the night before. Those dreams and images from Monday night had left me confused and tired. As a matter of fact, they made me so tired that I took the morning off from school and slept in. My body and mind just needed to recover after taking that horrendous beating.

I arrived at school in the afternoon and was shocked by what I found. The school was almost completely quiet, as if it was a morgue. There was no laughter in the halls. No one was joking around. I had spent so much time isolating myself in the Little Theater that I had failed to see the whole picture. It wasn't just me and my friends that had been affected by Chad's death. It was the entire school. Sure, my class and my group of friends had been influenced the most, but everyone had been touched in some way, shape, or form. I was beginning to see the larger perspective of the situation. Chad's death really did change the entire school.

Then I made my way to the Little Theater where I would discover all my friends and a few people I didn't know. I walked in. "Hey guys, how ya doing?"

"We're all right. You?"

"I've been better. Who are those people over there?" I pointed off in the direction of the chairs on the far side of the room. The lighting was dark since it was a theater, but my friends could see exactly who I was looking at.

"We don't know. As far as we can figure just some more dirtballs taking advantage of the situation so that they can get out of class."

Boy did that piss me off.

It was terrible. I could not understand people being so stuck on themselves and set on cutting classes that they would come here. My place to hide from the rest of the school had temporarily been taken away. It was so hard for me to accept that those kids were being allowed in our little spot, but slowly I learned just to ignore them. I began to talk to my friends and found out some interesting stories. Earlier in the day, when I had been sleeping, the funeral home director came to explain the evening to us. I was so angry with myself. That would have been my chance to learn more about funerals, and I missed it to catch up on sleep that I would never totally get caught up on. I grilled my friends for all that the director said.

The day continued to go by gradually, and I heard another story that angered me more than seeing those people in the Little Theater. I found out that there were people walking around the school that had the nerve to say things like, "I'm glad Chad's dead. He deserved to die. What a dumb shit." I heard stories like this, and I wanted to get up and find the people who said these things so that I could seriously hurt them. My friend had just died, and people were saying that they were happy that he was dead. It was appalling; why would people say such things? I made myself believe that the unattainable answer to this question was locked into the same reason Chad killed himself.

Then the question of "Why?" crept back into my head, and the mixed emotions came back again. I took a step forward and tried talking to some of the counselors. They explained to me that it was normal to feel the way I did. I could not understand what was normal about it. One of my best friends died, and I couldn't even cry. I felt like I was the one who should be dead.

The Funeral

The evening of Chad's funeral finally arrived. The struggle I had to release my feelings seemed to be never-ending. I was lost. I couldn't cry, and I couldn't accurately express the feelings that I had to anyone, including those that were close to me. I was only able to sit and stare out across the horizon, admiring the beauty and fragility of the world. Each person can make a difference, and with that change, the world can become a better place to live. What would happen to the piece of the world that Chad had been responsible for changing?

The time to leave for the church arrived, and my mom offered to drive me if I didn't feel up to it. I, of course, was too proud to say that I needed her to drive me, so instead, I lied and said that I felt fine. That was a mistake. I had not yet acknowledged my situation. I felt like it was still a horrible dream, or worse, a horrible joke. My mom made sure that I was alright once again before leaving with my brother. I waited thirty minutes or so before I left too. When I arrived, the reality of the situation slowly began to set in.

I made it to the church and could not help thinking to myself, "I don't want to be here." The images of the past funerals I attended seemed to be parts of one gigantic blurry dream. I drove around, attempting to find a parking spot. There were so many cars. It looked as if the whole town had shown up. I parked the car a good two or three blocks from the church, the only open place that I could find. As I walked towards the church, I saw waves of people coming and going. Those that were arriving were sad and quiet, while those that were leaving had tears streaming from their eyes. "It is a bad joke. I know Chad is alive and laughing," was all I could think. This is what I had forced myself to believe for the past few days, and it felt like an easy way to deal with things. Now I was seeing that it really wasn't a dream, but I did not want to admit it. There was no way that one of my friends could be lying in a casket.

The air was crisp and cool, biting at my face as I walked down the street. The church finally came into sight. It was unbelievable! There was a line of people leading out the door and down the block waiting to view Chad's body.

I found my brother and mom in line in an attempt to bypass some of the people. When we stepped foot in the church's foyer, I began to get a little scared. It was so crowded, and I felt like I couldn't breathe, as if the tears of all my friends were raining down on me and drowning me. Everyone looked as if the life had been taken out of them.

It was real, but it couldn't be happening to me, to this town, to my friends. The deathly feeling was too much for my little brother. He left with my mom without even getting one final glimpse of Chad. He had only known Chad as a friend of mine, but even he was affected so much this destructive act. There was no escaping it.

There was no place to run and no place to hide. My fears were racing at me full speed, and I had to meet them or forever be in pain. I skipped ahead in the line so that I wouldn't be alone, joined some of my friends, and we waited together.

The viewing line started to move slower and slower, which allowed my mind to wander. When I first entered the building, I had received a little card that was a remembrance of Chad. I clutched mine nervously. I couldn't stop shaking, and it scared me. I glanced at my card in hope of finding comfort. It stated the day he was born and the day he died, and it contained a brief message to him from his parents:

Chad, our son,
you are not forgotten,
nor will you ever be. As long
as life and memory last
we will remember you.
We miss you now, our hearts
are sore. As time goes by
we'll miss you
MORE.
Your loving smile,
your gentle face,
no one can fill your
VACANT place.

The card explains the reality of what was truly happening. My friend was really dead. The time had come to leave the foyer area and enter the church. Immediately upon entering the church, I felt momentarily free from all the sorrows of the past couple of days. However, that immediate feeling of relief left me when I began to look around the church. I saw the soccer team sitting together, all in tears. I finally had reached the point of understanding why they were crying, but for some reason, I just could not let go. As I slowly wandered down the aisle of that church, all the confusing thoughts of the past few days rushed through my head. Images popped up with those memories, images of teenagers dealing with a problem that shouldn't be forced upon them.

Walking down the church aisle with those thoughts and memories was the longest and most frightening walk of my life. It was nearing the beginning of the service. I looked behind me. There was still a line that went out the church waiting to see Chad. I couldn't believe how many people he had touched. I made it within ten feet of the casket, and I knew the moment of truth was going to arrive any minute. Before that moment came, however, I stopped to say hi to Chad's little brother. I caught a glimpse of his face. He had this puppy-dog look that showed all the pain and sorrow that he had experienced in the past few days. Then he said something to me, but I didn't hear what he said because I was overcome by the expression on his face. I only stood there. What I heard may have been different from his actual words, but I saw his lips move, and what I heard was, "Don't ever let your little brother down like Chad let me down."

What I had heard or imagined out of the mouth of Chad's little brother sent shivers up and down my spine. His expression looked as if his face and body were ready to explode from the events of the weekend. That expression made me want to cry, but I still couldn't let go of my feelings. The tears still would not come.

I stumbled forward, ready to face Chad's corpse. Again I

stopped, but this time to talk to Chad's parents. The conversation was short, but it is something I will always remember. They said, "Thanks for being Chad's friend. When you go back towards the foyer of the church, you'll be able to find some photos of you and Chad together." I wanted to say something to comfort them, to take their heartache and mine away at the same time, but the words were not there. I just smiled briefly and headed for the coffin.

The shivers that I had felt when talking to his little brother had come back. This time they were more intense, almost as if my spine was going to crack.

The moment of truth had arrived. It was the moment I had dreaded for days . . . the moment I had dreaded my entire life.

The doubts that I had all my life popped into my mind: What is God? Is there a God? What happens to people when they die? Why do people have to die?

It was time to pay my respects. It was time to observe Chad's corpse. I walked up to the coffin and took a quick look. Chad was lying there, a soccer ball on one side, surrounded by all different types of flowers. He looked so cold and stiff. It wasn't the Chad in my memories, the Chad that was on the remembrance card. His body looked fake, as if someone had tried to forge his identity. He wasn't smiling. He was dead; it seemed like he wasn't even there. He didn't look real. He just lay there.

I had a quick flashback to the summer before our freshman year. Chad and I had just finished lifting weights together, and we were walking across the gym floor, getting ready to go to the locker room. We were talking about the upcoming year, the year when we would first enter high school. I said, "I can't wait to play football. It's something I've never done. I hope it's fun."

He turned to me and said, "Don't tell the coach, but I'm going to play soccer instead of football." He was so excited. His face showed a youthful determination, and it gleamed full of life and happiness.

Tears began to stream from my eyes. That look into the coffin only lasted two or three seconds, but to me it felt like an eternity. I was staring at the face of death, the face of all my fears. It is an image I'll never forget. That was all the time I could take. Other people had to pay their respects so that the service could start. But I think the real reason that I didn't take a longer look was because I couldn't handle seeing one of my friends lying in a wooden box in a church unknown to me.

As I turned from the coffin, more memories of Chad jumped into my head. Memories of the two of us attending the same Lutheran day school as children. We had been good friends who had competed against each other and created memories together, but now those days had ended. The good times and bad times that we had spent together in the past were over and would only live on in the memories he left behind.

Chad was really dead.

It was so hard to believe. Faced with this fact, the tears that had refused to come for days now came like a waterfall.

I wanted to run down the aisle and escape out the back of the church. Then I would be able to hide from the pain and the finality of the funeral. However, I walked down the aisle of the church, attempting to regain the composure I had faked the past few days. I made it to the end of the aisle and found the bulletin board with the pictures that his parents had told me about. It seemed ironic. I was being attacked by Chad's death from all sides. I had just seen him dead, lacking all life as I knew it, and now I was looking at pictures showing Chad full of life. Chad, in the photos, was the way I had remembered him: alive and ready for anything. I looked at one picture in particular. The tears that had tried to sneak out moments earlier again flowed uncontrollably, like a never-ending river of grief. My body had fought the tears for days, and they finally won their way out.

The picture was of a birthday party Chad threw when we were in the fifth or sixth grade. I didn't remember much about that party. The picture showed Chad aiming a slingshot at the camera. I traced through my memory and found that picture. We had raided his kitchen cabinets before he opened his gifts, and after he received the slingshot, we immediately went outside, and he practiced with it.

This picture and the memories that it held once again echoed to me that a close friend of mine, one whom I had partied and talked with and had been friends with since we were little kids, was truly dead. He had died by his own hand by a piece of worthless metal. He had died by the iron and lead that was destroying the world we live in and changing it every day. This picture of Chad started to blur from the tears that filled my eyes.

I continued to look at the other pictures of Chad through my tears, pictures of him with all his friends. He's gone. He's really gone. I noticed other pictures of us together as little kids. Until this point, I had forgotten what good friends we had been when we were younger. The pain of his death seemed to increase even more now.

I was finally able to experience the anguish of his separation from the world as my friends had over the past few days. My feelings were finally coming out. The tears felt like they would never stop.

I ran from the churning torment inside and found refuge in the arms of a friend. He had already experienced the outburst of emotion I was feeling. He gave me a hug and told me to let it all out. He hadn't been a close friend, but now my relationships with every individual I knew were closer.

I cried and cried. I began to gain a little composure, but the tears kept coming.

He released me and let me stand on my own. It was weird. I was finally able to cry, and it seemed there was no way I would be able to stop crying.

I took a seat in the balcony for the beginning of the service. I could see the whole church, and I'll never forget how crowded it was. Even in the balcony, I felt crowded for space, but somehow it made me feel safer and stronger. I felt a unity with each individual because I knew that they were experiencing the same mixed emotions I felt.

It was time for the funeral to begin. I was so shaken up that the funeral itself no longer seemed scary to me, due in part to the camaraderie in the balcony. The service began with a hymn and then the closing of the casket. As the casket was closed, the people in that church shed enough tears to fill Lake Michigan.

It was final. None of us would ever see Chad again. He was sealed away from me and the rest of the world, where nothing would ever reach him.

The service continued with Chad's favorite song, "Glory of Love" by Peter Cetera. It was weird because I had never known Chad to listen to this song. The chills that traveled up and down my spine controlled my body once again. This time they made me feel paralyzed.

Much of the rest of the service is a blur to me. Several times I left the service to get some fresh air or to regain my composure. I would go outside and stare into the sky.

The service ended with Chad's family leading the way as his coffin was carried out of the church. The pallbearers were all friends of Chad's who had been really close to him. It was difficult to watch them carry him. They were trying so hard to hold back their tears. Once the service ended, I did not want to go home.

I felt it a necessity to hang out and talk with my friends, and when I found out that one friend of mine was having a few people over, I decided to go downstairs and talk to Chad's parents once more before I went to that friend's house. They were down in the fellowship hall, and I asked them if they would allow me to take the picture of Chad's birthday party, one of my greatest memories of Chad. They agreed, and it is something I will always cherish.

I caught up with my friends at the house, and we sat around and talked about the way things were in the present, about past experiences with Chad, and about what the future would be like without him. It was amazing the way our town had bonded together over the past few days. We ordered some pizza, and when we went to get it, we found out that it was free. The store said that it was the least they could do.

Later, I found out that we could all go to another friend's house for the rest of the night, which sounded like something I needed, but when I called home, my mom said I needed sleep and gave me a certain time to be home. Before I left, I gave a few people rides back to their houses. I was willing to do anything to help my friends out, and they would do the same for me.

After I arrived home, I sat and talked with my mom for about a half hour before going to bed. I think it was because I still feared going to sleep. My dreams held too many demons, goblins, and memories.

Part II: Mending

Wistful Wednesday

I woke up feeling worse than I had all week. I felt run-down instead of feeling alive, and I couldn't understand why. My sleep that evening lacked any dreams. There were no images of Chad running through my mind. I had been engulfed in complete darkness all night. I had felt at total peace, but now something did not seem right.

I arrived at school five minutes late, back on my daily schedule, and only saw a handful of people as I walked through the halls. Everyone was in class. I went to class and attempted to study, but I just could not do it. It felt like something was blocking me from ever studying again. I wanted to go to the Little Theater because after the funeral, I was beginning to understand how I felt, and I needed someone to talk to.

However, students were no longer allowed to go to the Little Theater. The administration felt it best that we start living our lives again, putting Chad's unfortunate incident into the past. As the school day went by, I was able to see many of my friends slowly getting back into their everyday lives.

On the outside, everyone appeared to have finally accepted Chad's death and dealt with it. I noticed that many of my friends were able to crack smiles for the first time in days.

My expression, though, would not change. I clung to the expressions of the past few days because I had just begun to accept Chad's death and would now have to deal with it. I was surprised and angered that everyone seemed to be getting over this event with ease. Don't get me wrong, there was a lot of pain. But it just felt to me that we should never be happy again. I had trouble with the idea that we should live our lives the way we always did.

My classes dragged by hour by hour. The teachers began to teach, and the students began to learn again. It was almost as if someone had paused our lives momentarily and now decided to force life to play on once again. I felt like I was one of the select few who was stuck on pause or accidently put into slow motion.

The silence that I had heard in the hallways the past few days was broken by the familiar sounds of classes. The student body had shown its sorrow and now was ready to heal. Slowly, with each passing hour, I accepted this sense of healing myself. As the day progressed, I felt as if someone was turning up my speed at a gradual pace. Seventh hour finally arrived, the second to last hour of the day. I was almost back to full speed, and it was a good thing because I had to go to my English class. This class was taught by a brilliant man who seemed to know everything, but at the conclusion of this hour, my opinion would change. I walked in as the bell sounded and took my seat in the second row on the right. I had the second seat, which was a good spot because I was able to hear all his lectures clearly and take good notes from this vantage point.

This is one hour out of the year that I will always want to forget. As a class, we were discussing the book The Catcher in the Rye. I had not finished it and have decided never to finish it. My teacher gave us a packet listing roughly twenty major themes from the book, and we would pick and choose what we were going to discuss. He, as all teachers, decided that today was a good day to start bringing us back to our everyday lives. He began his lecture that day, and for some reason beyond my comprehension, he chose the topic of suicide.

He explained how suicide was shown as a major part of the book. The topic that would resurrect pain for all of us was explained. He told us stories in detail of the different ways people would go about killing themselves. It was horrible. I just put my head down and tried not to listen to what he had to say. At times I raised my head to look at the rest of the class. There were many kids like me who just put their heads down, while others went into tears. This man, who had so much respect in my eyes before, now had none. I wanted to get up and tell him to shut the hell up, or better yet, I just wanted to get up, walk out, and never come back.

For some reason I didn't. Maybe I was too weak or maybe I was just afraid. I don't know.

The bell sounded, and we all raced for the door. We had to escape this sickening hour. Many of my fellow classmates immediately went to the administration office to demand that something be done.

I just went to my next class, and I have no memory of that class period. My mind was someplace else entirely. I think my teacher was able to sense that, because he asked me to stay after class. He told me that the best thing I could do for myself was to put this event behind me, but keep it in my memories, and that I couldn't allow such a dreadful incident to screw up my life. I knew he was right, but it was just so difficult to do.

That evening when I arrived home from football practice, my mom and dad sat me down and talked to me. They told me the same basic message that my teacher had told me: "Put it behind you."

I wandered over to the TV and tried to lose my feelings in the screen in front of me, but it was no use. The phone rang. It was my brother calling from college to see how I was doing. I picked up the telephone and explained to him the details of what exactly had occurred. Even though he had been in town recently, he left before getting a chance to talk with me. I told him the gruesome details over the phone and almost broke down in tears. The amount of pain and sadness inside of me was still too much. After my conversation, I went back to the TV as a way to try to hide some of my emotions. My parents walked over and said good night, restating the fact that I had to put everything behind me.

Putting this event behind me was something that I thought about all night, and something that crept into my dreams.

The Horror Continues

I dragged my body up the staircase that evening like I was carrying two ten-ton suitcases. I was exhausted and felt completely empty inside. Life was worthless, and somehow it would never be able to conquer death. I was more confused than I had been all week. All day and all week, the only thing I had heard was how terrible Chad's suicide was, but the same people who had been telling me this all week were now telling me that I had to forget what had just happened to me and to the rest of the town. and that I had to start living my life for myself again and put my memories of Chad into the back of my mind.

I had tried so hard to do this all week, and I now understood that no matter what anyone told me, I couldn't do it. Or maybe I didn't want to do it. I had been so close to Chad and then had become so distant from him. Now I was as close to him as I had ever been in my entire life, and I didn't want to try to destroy that newfound closeness. This made me angry.

I was angry at Chad for putting me in such an awkward position.

I was angry at myself for forgetting the closeness that Chad and I once had.

I was angry at myself for refusing to accept the reality of the world and the events that occurred within that reality. I had not been able to deal with it this whole week, but the events of this week pointed out to me that I had not been able to deal with it my entire life.

I was angry at my mom and all the other important adults in my life for telling me things I didn't want to hear, even though I had to hear them.

I was angry at the world, in general, for creating problems like this. They were too great for me or anyone to handle.

All this anger churned inside of me until it bloomed into hate. I hated myself for the way I had acted all week and all my life. Every time someone close to me died, I had somehow turned my back on the situation.

This week I had been able to face the tormenting circumstances, but I hated myself for taking so long to accomplish it.

I hated every important person in my life for not giving me any advice, and then I seemed to hate them even more when they did.

I hated Chad for what he had done to me and all our friends.

I felt hypocritical. In one day, I had gone from being at his funeral crying and mourning his death to hating him and wishing that he was alive so I could beat the living hell out of him. I had been fighting a war with my feelings all week, and I realized it was a war I could not win.

I turned on my radio so that I could hear some comforting music and calm down. I wanted my body to relax and take a break from all these emotional wars. Anger was overwhelming me. I sat down on the couch in my room. It was a very ugly dark brown color and always felt like it was going to fall apart, but it never did.

The radio announcer had been mumbling, and now he stopped as he put on the next song. It was "It's So Hard To Say Goodbye To Yesterday." I began to cry again. I sat there painfully listening to every word of that song. It was so real; every word applied to me, to my feelings over Chad. It was like a terrible torture that would not end. There was something inside of me that screamed to turn the radio off, but there was an even louder voice that drowned the other one out. It said that this song was something I needed to hear because even though it made me feel terrible, when it was over, I would feel just a little bit better about myself and the events of the weekend. The song would not let me ever forget him, and that's what made it so special to me. I sat there thinking about how much I wanted to forget Chad and throw him out of my life forever. At the same time, though, I wanted to always remember him and never stop thinking about him, because as soon as I stopped thinking about him, he truly would be gone.

Reasoning like this, I rummaged through my tape collection and searched for my tape with this song on it. I sat there on that ugly brown couch in the middle of that ugly brown attic of a room listening to that same song over and over again. I must have listened to the song for over a half-hour, but to me it felt like both seconds and an eternity. All I thought about was how I could possibly gather the courage to say goodbye to one of my friends as all the adults in my life were telling me to. It was something I didn't want to do, and I wasn't even sure I should do.

Slowly, the courage began to course through my veins, and I pushed the memories to the back of my mind. It was so hard, but everyone told me that it was something I had to do for my own emotional and physical health.

As I did this, I started to feel more relaxed and relieved, but I also felt reckless because I was trying to abandon a friend of mine. This soon changed to a feeling of guilt. At the same time, I began to feel renewed, yet the new energy locked me in chains. Life seemed to once again circulate through my blood, but I felt like I no longer knew how to use it.

I was ready to go to sleep. I lunged off the couch and crawled over to the bed. For the first time all week, I felt alive and awake in my mind. The fog that clouded my mind had disappeared, but my body felt weak and exhausted.

I climbed into my waterbed, making a crash landing. The waves created a swoosh sound as they went from side to side. The waterbed became my oasis where I could lie down and avoid my problems, my guilt, my pain, and my suffering. I looked at the alarm clock and noticed that it was two in the morning. The red lights seemed to talk to me and tell me something I didn't want to hear, so I turned over and looked outside. It was complete darkness. All I could see was one giant picture of black. I heard the crickets chirping, but they didn't seem to be chirping as loudly as they had in the past. The waves from the lake were splashing against the rocks on the shoreline, and the wind seemed to be howling louder than it ever had before. The sounds were all so beautiful and peaceful, yet they also felt so real and scary. It was as if I was trapped between two worlds and I couldn't get out of either one of them.

I slowly dozed off to the sounds of the peaceful outdoors and drifted away into my dreams, the one place I hadn't been safe all week.

I awoke to see myself lying peacefully in the bed. It was almost as if I was looking down at myself from the ceiling of my room. I began to toss and turn as if I was trying to fight somebody or something. Then I saw myself wake up and look outside the window into the darkness, but for some reason I was unable to get up. All I could see was my reflection; my bed had been walled off on all sides by a mirrors. It was as if I had been isolated in a room where everything could be seen and nothing could be hidden.

Each mirror portrayed a different image of me. The one straight ahead made me out to be a short, fat kid. I looked like a Goodyear blimp. The one to my left made me look like a tall skinny kid who was dying of hunger, and the other two mirrors portrayed images of the way I was seen by the people around me and by the way I saw myself. It was scary, like I was at a carnival and people were staring at me and laughing. My face was worn out and beaten up; the mirror reflected how I saw myself. It looked like I had fought a boxing match and lost. My eyes were all puffy and red, and I had scrapes and gashes on my face as if someone had taken a spoon and carved into my skin. I appeared to be in so much pain.

Then I looked at the way society saw me, and I was a handsome young adult. There was nothing wrong with me. I looked like any other teenager from any other part of the country.

I closed my eyes. This was all too much to bear. I reopened them to check whether the carnival-type atmosphere was still there. It wasn't. All the mirrors now portrayed the image society saw of me, the perfectly healthy young adult.

I quickly turned around because I felt like someone was watching me or trying to sneak up on me. The paranoia allowed me to catch a glimpse of a man who had been staring at me from outside the window. He disappeared into a fog before I was able to study him.

Then I turned and faced forward. Chad was standing at the foot of my bed in a cloud of fog. He had a puppy-dog look on his face, and he was very hard to see, as if he was fading into the fog and yet still heading straight for me. His blond hair and patented grin grabbed me as I noticed a path of blood leading out of the fog. I tried to say something, but I couldn't speak. My mouth moved, but no words would come out. Chad moved a little further out of the fog. He looked so pale and weak, and he seemed to be wrapped up in big chains, the kind you see on anchors of battleships. It was as if he were the anchor on a battleship. His blue eyes no longer sparkled as they had so often in the past. I continued to try to speak, but it was no use. My body just would not let me. He stood there staring at me with a disappointed look on his face. He then said something that ripped me into a thousand pieces. "Why are you trying to forget me?"

I wanted to say that I didn't want to, but that I had to. I wanted to reach out, but I was paralyzed. I was helpless, left only with the chance to sit there and stare at him as he repeated, "Why are you trying to forget me?"

He started to fade away, and he mumbled something about never forgetting friends, never. The fog engulfed him and stole him out of my sight. I also could faintly hear the words, "Chains are never broken, only enlarged," words that were getting drowned out by the song "Glory of Love." This song was taking over every thought in my mind. It began to get louder and louder.

My body popped up in a cold sweat, and I looked around, panicked. I was scared and confused. There were no longer any chains, any mirrors, or any images of Chad. I was left lying there with new questions arising in my mind. "Chad, where did you go? What chains can't be broken? And why can't those chains be broken?

Will I ever be able to live a normal life again?"

I looked around my room at the pennants and the blue drapes hanging on the wall. The Packer pennant seemed to be changing colors, and the badger in the Wisconsin pennant was grinding its teeth at me. The crickets began to chirp, "It's So Hard To Say Goodbye To Yesterday."

I knew that this was going to be a long night. The area of my dreams had once again proved itself as unsafe territory for me.

I lay in bed questioning all the knowledge that I once felt I had. I wasn't sure who I should listen to.

Were my parents right or was Chad? It was an inescapable question with a very difficult answer. Before I was able to come to my solution, I discovered many things about myself. I asked myself, "Is there really a God?" Then I answered, "I hope not, otherwise I'll never see Chad again." Then I started to rethink, and I discovered that if there wasn't a God, I probably would never see Chad anyway, or maybe if I did, I wouldn't know him. My beliefs, the ones that had been taught to me for years, were in question. I was left with many challenging questions that had no answers, or answers which were impossible to accept.

That evening, I attempted to face my fears, but all I did was create new ones about where I had come from and what my purpose was. To me, it seemed Chad's purpose was to affect every one of our lives and make us ask tough questions, and I wanted to avoid them, but I knew that the longer I avoided them, the more they would sneak into my dreams and destroy my life and mind. On this night, I was unable to find the solutions I was searching for, but I had to discover them soon or I would face one eternal nightmare for the rest of my life.

Thursday

The next morning rolled around, and I found my head implanted in my pillow. I had no intention of leaving my bed because I was so tired. My dreams had kept me awake for many hours during the night, yet I still somehow managed to get a couple hours of sleep. My dad came into my room and told me that it was time for me to get up and get ready for school. I lay there saying that I didn't want to go and that I needed more sleep.

He responded, "Get up. You slept in once this week, and you can't afford to miss this much school. You've got to start getting back on your regular schedule."

No matter how much I didn't want to admit it, I knew he was right. The only way I could continue to heal was to begin living my life the way I always had.

I rolled off the edge of my bed and felt the pain of hitting the floor. The brown carpet scraped my face, and the red light from my alarm clock spoke to me. I looked a little closer at the numbers on the clock and was able to see that I was running five minutes behind my normal schedule. I quickly raced down the stairs into the shower. It felt so good to get rid of the grimy feeling that I had all week. Momentarily, there in the shower, I felt like my old self: no problems or worries, aside from the fact that I was extremely late for school.

I rushed up the stairs after brushing my teeth, changed into my clothes for that school day, grabbed my wallet and my keys, and flew out the door. I sped to school, and when I arrived, I was already ten minutes late. My friends were hanging out in the commons, but the teacher wouldn't let me in because I was late, so I went to my locker, gathered my books, and slowly walked to study hall. Since I was already late and was unable to hang out in the commons, I took my time getting to study hall. I really didn't feel like doing any homework.

Lethargically, I walked into study hall and went over to the teacher. "There was this huge train, and I was stuck at the railroad track for like ten minutes." He looked at me, smiled, and said, "You can do better than that," then told me to take my seat. I smiled because I knew my excuse had been lousy and then attempted to get started on my homework.

I sat down and actually was able to put together a few minutes and a few thoughts to get some studying done. I was so proud of myself. However, before I really got anything accomplished, the bell sounded, and it was time for me to go to my next class.

I arrived at algebra class with that quote still staring at me. "It is never too late to be what you might have been." We had a substitute teacher and were supposed to work on a certain assignment. Instead of doing that, I talked with the girl that sat next to me for a long time.

We talked about how weird the school was without Chad. Nothing seemed real anymore, but at the same time everything seemed too real. She had always had every answer, but now she was lost like me. I remember scrambling at the end of the period to copy the work I was supposed to have been working on. Luckily, I was able to copy it and turn it in so that I wouldn't get in trouble the next day for screwing around.

The rest of the morning dragged on like a blurry cloud. I don't remember much except that I was finally able to start studying again, and slowly I began to realize what everyone meant when they said, "Put it behind you." There is one thing that specifically stands out about that foggy day. I spoke to a teacher with a couple of fellow students about what had happened in our English class on Wednesday. As long as I've had teachers, I have never known one to be as outraged as she was. She said that the teacher who did this was stupid and deserved to be fired immediately. This teacher was so outraged that she made it a point to write something down so that she would remember to talk to the administration. She kept saying, "You just don't do things like that. He should be more intelligent than that." She was saying what each of us students were thinking. Of course, there were also many students like me who were torn. On one hand, we weren't ready to go that far, but thought it was necessary that some kind of disciplinary action be taken, but we also felt he should answer for the pain he caused all of us.

It was time to eat lunch. I sat down with a bunch of my friends, and we finally were starting to have normal conversations, making jokes, and saying stupid things to make each other feel better. Things were appearing to become normal again. Lunch came to an end, and I was afraid of that. I wanted lunch to last forever so that I wouldn't have to go to my English class. I started talking to one of my friends about skipping the next hour, and he said that we wouldn't have to because the teacher was gone. I asked, "He's been fired already?"

"No, I don't think so. All I know is that we have a sub today. We'll skip out tomorrow so that we don't have to listen to that man."

I felt a little bit relieved, but I still thought that this teacher was going to be there and the sub was just a hopeful rumor. I walked into class and saw the substitute teacher. Relief surged through my blood. A lady who looked like another teacher and the principal sat in chairs next to the substitute. We went from a horrendous day in class to a day that looked like it was going to be just as bad.

We now had two teachers and a principal. I turned to a friend and asked what was going on. He responded, "Apparently, aside from you and me, the whole class either went to the administration and complained or called them. I guess they took a lot of heat from students as well as parents, but that's all I know. They probably want to kill this before the whole community hears about it."

The bell sounded, and we all took our seats. The substitute introduced himself and told us that our teacher was at a meeting and that he would be back on Friday. That took care of the idea that he was fired, but then why were this lady and our principal in the room?

"Now, I am going to turn you over to the principal because he has something very important he wants to discuss with you."

The principal stood up and addressed us. "Class, it has come to my attention through many of you and your parents that something happened in here yesterday that should not have happened. Am I right?"

"Yes," the class hesitantly replied.

"I am here to try and fix that the best I can. I really can't do much. That is why I brought the school psychologist along. She is much better equipped to deal with such a situation, and I'll just monitor and listen to the conversation, throwing in what little help I can offer."

I didn't even know we had a school psychologist. She basically told us her impression of what she heard had happened and asked if we had any comments to add. Students popped up from all over the room adding little things. Then some other people started to change the topic to the fact that everything he taught was about death.

This angered me, so I put in my two cents' worth. "I don't think it's the fact that all the material he teaches deals with death. I can handle that. What I have a problem with is the fact that many of us had finally begun to deal with Chad's suicide, and then he brought it back in front of our faces in such a gruesome manner. It just isn't right or fair."

The psychologist then asked me, "Do you think our conversation today is going to help you put this behind you?"

I replied, "I hope so, because I had finally started to deal with it at the funeral, and now it's as real as ever."

The conversation between her and our class lasted the entire hour when it was only expected to last ten or fifteen minutes. I don't think they believed it was as severe a problem as it actually was, but now they had an understanding of the situation and realized that it was much more complex than they imagined. One thing about that period angered me. The substitute teacher asked if he could say something and, of course, anyone that wanted to say anything spoke. He said, "I think it's kind of unfair of you guys to grill him like this when he isn't even here to defend himself. It sounds like a mutiny to me where everyone takes a shot at the teacher because they have a chance to."

I sat there thinking to myself, "You are a **** idiot. You just don't understand the grief we're feeling, do you?"

However, I didn't say anything, but I think this guy understood that it wasn't like he said, because as soon as he said it, he received about twenty dirty looks.

The bell rang, and it was the end of another period of school. I was starting to feel better. I thought about finding that psychologist and telling her about some of my dreams, but I figured that if she was a school psychologist that I didn't even know we had, how good could she be?

Consequently, I continued on with the rest of my day. During the final hour of school, I was even able to crack a smile after my history teacher told our class a joke. It wasn't necessarily that the joke was funny, but it was the way the teacher told it that cheered me up.

Football practice that day was the same as it had been all week. I tried and tried to hit people really hard, but I just could not do it. After practice, the coach talked to me and once again told me that I had to put this incident behind me and deal with my own life. He told me that the next day, I would have to play one of my best games of the year because it would determine whether or not I would make all-conference. I went home that evening wondering if I would ever be able to regain my composure on the field as I was beginning to in the classroom. It was so confusing and so very hard to do.

Thursday Evening

I went home that evening wondering if I would ever regain that status that I had once possessed on the athletic field and in the classroom. I was making progress, but everything still seemed so worthless. I could still perform as I was supposed to, but I lacked the desire to do anything right now.

I went home that evening and discussed my inability to put the week behind me with my parents. They told me that it was a tough thing to do, but it was something I had to do. I couldn't help thinking, "What do you know? You're only my parents. You don't feel the same way I do."

Then my mom said, "I know we can never understand what you're feeling. What we can understand is the fact that we see you ripping yourself apart inside. Chad's death is affecting all the things you have worked so hard for over the years. Your grades and your off-field activities are suffering. It's a hard thing to do and is something we luckily never had to deal with. However, you haven't been so lucky, and now it is up to you to mature faster than you're supposed to."

My mom had just stated everything that I had been feeling in my confused little mind. How could she do something like that? However she did it, it alerted me to the fact that I had to put Chad behind me once and for all. The way to do that was not to forget him or push him out of my mind. What I had to do was as simple as what that teacher had told me on Sunday evening. I had to go on living my life the way I always had, holding on to my memories, but not trying to relive those memories.

It seemed like too simple an answer for such a huge problem. It was hard to believe.

I decided to give it a shot.

I rummaged through my closets and found a bunch of old black wristbands that I had never worn before but had bought anyway. I took them down to the kitchen, found a bottle of Wite-Out, and took the Wite-Out and sat down in front of the TV. There, with the help of my little brother, I applied the Wite-Out to the black wristbands. We initialed each one C.M. and also labeled them with Chad's soccer number. It was my small way of saying that Chad would always be with me.

As time has worn on, these initials have worn off each and every wristband, but I still wear the wristband as a remembrance of him. After we got done making these extraordinary wristbands, I lay down and watched some TV. It was the first time all week that I was able to relax and lie in front of the TV after all I had done during the week. But now it felt like I was wasting my time. I understood that every individual only has so much time in a day, and it seemed wrong for me to spend mine lying around on a couch. It was so comfortable on this night, though, that I felt it was something I needed to do. I allowed my fatigue from the week to catch up with me. I was exhausted mentally and physically and needed to get some rest before my football game the next day.

I went to bed early that night, around ten o'clock or so. It felt so nice to be able to go to bed at a normal time . . . until I thought about the images that might face me in my dreams.

I was freezing that evening. It must have been five or ten degrees, and I tried to warm up by cranking up the heat on my waterbed and thinking of someplace warm. I fell asleep thinking of the way it was around my house in the summer, the hundred-degree weather and the heat that burned my skin. I thought about things like swimming parties, and I even dreamt about having one.

In the dream, I had all my close friends over, and we had a grill-out where we cooked brats, and we were skiing, swimming, and tubing on the lake. After we finished using the boat, we drank beer. My parents weren't home. All I knew was that I was holding a nice summer party when we all decided to go swimming again. I slammed my beer and flew down the hill, jumping off the pier into the water. It felt so cool and refreshing. I swam out to a raft that was roughly twenty yards from the end of the pier, and once I made it to the raft, I looked out at the lake. It was perfectly calm and so beautiful. A fish jumped occasionally, and a few fishermen off in the distance were catching fish.

The world was working the way it always did in the summer. The island off to my right looked as beautiful and calm as the water. Nobody was on the lake or the island because it was a weekday and most people had to work.

In the distance, where the water passed between the island and the mainland, I was able to see a buoy that said, "Slow No Wake." No boats could travel through this area and disrupt it by making waves. This part of the lake looked like a piece of glass. I turned my head and glanced back at my house. My friends were cooking brats and listening to the radio.

I was ready to jump back into the water and head back to join them when I decided to take a final view of the lake. I looked towards the area where I had seen the "Slow No Wake" sign.

It was gone.

I turned around, and it was right next to the raft. It changed forms on me now.

Instead of being a buoy, it turned into my uncle who had died very recently. I had a unique bond with him, and I missed him.

He said to me, "So you finally are able to deal with my death."

I responded, "I think so. I understand that I miss you and that you will never truly be gone as long as I have a heart."

"Exactly. You finally did learn, and I suppose you understand what attending my funeral could have done for you?"

"Yeah. I think I've learned."

"Then I believe you have finally taken the step you needed to take, and I can go."

"Don't go!" I cried.

"Don't worry, I'll always be with you."

With those words, the buoy reappeared and my uncle was gone. I sat there for a moment before deciding to lie down in the sun. I fell asleep for what felt like a year and woke up to find Chad beside me on the raft. "Chad, is that you?"

"Yes."

He found me again, but this time I was finally able to speak with him. "How have you been?"

He responded that death was treating him well, then asked how I was doing.

I looked at him and said, "Fine."

"Come on, tell me the truth."

I paused a moment, trying to find the right words to initiate a conversation with his ghostly presence, "Okay, I've been doing lousy all week. I just can't escape the torture that you've been putting me through with your death. It's so hard to accept and even harder to put behind me. Why did you do it? Was it something I did or said?" I waited as I tried to read his reaction.

His face stayed stoic and left me no clues, no answers. It was the story of this whole day, week, and experience. After a long pause, he started to respond. "The reason why I did it is unimportant. What matters is that I made the mistake, and it is irreversible."

"You mean you think it was a mistake?"

"I don't think, I know, but the Lord allows everyone a mistake every once in a while."

"What's that supposed to mean?"

"I can't tell you. All I can say is that you have to follow what's inside your heart in everything you do. Don't listen to your mind because that can be corrupted by the world. Your heart knows your only true feeling, and it will always guide you to the right place. I stopped listening to my heart, and look at what happened to me."

A moment of silence lingered as I thought of the right words, the right question to respond. There was only one that really mattered. "Will I ever see you again?"

"I doubt it. I just came back to tell you that you are once again traveling down the right path. You will stray every once in a while, but as long as you always come back to that path, you will be alright."

He paused for a moment, looked off into the distance, and appeared to be in a world of his own. Then he stated in a distant low voice that could barely be heard, "Well, I've got to go."

"Don't!"

"I have to. You don't want to disobey what the Man upstairs says more than once."

"What do you mean, more than once?"

"Do you think I should really be here talking to you? Well, I'll see you later."

"I'll always miss you and remember you, Chad."

With this, Chad disappeared, and I was left sleeping on the raft. Then I felt this terrible cold water splashing me. I had just been hit by a water balloon. I jumped up, got into the water, swam back to shore, and ate a brat that my friends had saved for me while I was sleeping on the raft. Everything seemed better now, and I was beginning to feel a peace within myself that I hadn't felt for a long time.

I woke up to somebody shaking me. It was my dad telling me that it was time to get up and go to school. I rolled over and saw that it was ten to seven; the day was Friday.

Friday

This was one of those days that I felt a need to continue hugging the pillow. I was so tired and so exhausted.

All my dad kept saying was, "Get up! Today's game day."

I heard those words, but I felt like there was no possible way for me to play football today. It felt like I had just finished a game and my body needed an endless amount of sleep.

My dad tugged on me so that I would be forced to climb out of bed.

I got up, but the world seemed so foggy, as if this were another bad dream and I was sleepwalking. I was in a daze that had an indescribably relaxing feeling. I trudged down to the bathroom and showered.

Since today was game day, the team had to dress up, so I threw on a shirt and tie. I even thought about wearing a jacket, but the jacket reminded me of homecoming weekend, and I did not want to be thinking about that all day. I made sure to wear a different shirt than I had less than a week ago and borrowed one of my dad's ties so that everything I wore would be different. The tie had an image of a fish, and its eyes stared at people when they stared at you. This was great because then I didn't have to put up with people constantly staring at me all day. They were too busy staring at my tie.

I climbed into my car and sped off to school. I walked in almost ten minutes late and was somehow able to sneak my way into the commons. It was nice to sit down and relax instead of going to study hall. I was able to begin changing my focus toward the game that evening.

That morning, one of my friends and I saw our English teacher walking in the halls, and we both immediately turned to each other. "What an asshole," I said. "He walks around like he did nothing wrong. It makes me sick."

Then my friend said, "Did you hear? He has to have a conversation with the principal today. He's in deep shit. He might get fired over that lecture the other day."

I said under my breath, "Really? That doesn't seem fair. He's a good teacher. He just made a mistake."

The rest of Friday is mostly a blur to me. I was thinking about so many things: school, the events of the past week, the game that I had to play later on that day. I do remember having this incredible feeling of nervousness. At the time I thought I was nervous about how I was going to perform in the upcoming game, but now that I look back on it, I think I was nervous because of the uncertainty of my future and the future of those around me. School had always felt like a waste of time to me, and it felt like that even more so after the past week. I had no idea what I liked to do, or why I even had to do anything at all. It was all so worthless. I just wanted to be left alone so that I could sit in a corner.

However, that would not happen. No one would leave me alone, teachers or students. It was the same thing all day. "Do you think you guys are going to win tonight? How's the morale of the team? What's practice been like all week?" It seemed as if everyone had already forgotten the past few days.

I acted like it didn't bother me, and I answered their questions, but pain grew inside of me. "How can you be so excited about one dumb, lousy football game? It's a meaningless game." If my coach had seen inside my head that day, I don't think he would have let me play. I didn't want to play. I debated all day about going to him and saying, "Coach, I don't feel up to it." For some reason, maybe lack of courage, I decided not to do it.

To this day, I think that I made one of the best decisions of my life by playing that game. I had to start living sometime, and what better time to start living than while playing football? I mean, let's face it, either I start to perform or I get my ass kicked.

The doubts continued all day for me. It was moments before my English class. I couldn't skip out because then I wouldn't be able to play that night, and I would really have the coach angry at me. I didn't want to go to class, but I really had no choice. I walked in, and for the second day in a row, I saw the principal sitting in the front of the room with a serious expression on his face. I looked around saw our regular teacher. That was when I knew that this was going to be an extremely long class period.

The bell rang, and the principal stood up to speak. "Class, it looks as though we have two sides to a story here, and we have got to come to some understanding." Whatever had occurred in the meeting earlier that morning was not the firing of our teacher. He continued, "I can't be sure of exactly what happened in here the other day, but after speaking to your teacher, I'm sure that the misunderstanding we had was unintentional. My job today is to patch up the misunderstanding. I would like you all to throw your complaints out in the open."

No one spoke, which I knew would happen. We weren't stupid. Our complaints would be heard and only lightly regarded, and then we would have to go through the rest of the year with that teacher blackballing us.

"Come on now, I was in here yesterday, and almost everyone had a complaint. This is the time to straighten out those complaints." No one raised their hands. "All right then, I guess it's up to me to throw out the first question. Sir, what response do you have over the complaint that the topic of discussion was wrong for this class the other day?"

The teacher spoke, "Well, I thought it was a pivotal part of the book that we were reading. At the time, it didn't seem to me that it was upsetting anyone."

"What about the girls that were crying in class, and those of us who stopped taking notes and just put our heads down?" someone in the back of the room shouted.

"I did not see anyone crying. If I had, I would have immediately switched to another topic. As for the complaint that students were putting their heads down and discontinuing note-taking, that happens every day, and I just thought some of you were not paying attention to the lecture as usual."

With those slick answers, he made the whole incident sound like a silly misunderstanding. I was now more confused than ever. I wasn't sure if we should believe him. The principal said, "Well, I'm glad we were able to get this whole problem cleared up."

"Wait," I said. "I still don't feel right, and considering the events of the past few days, I don't think I'll ever be able to feel right when talking about this book or this topic. I know I can never read this book. It's just too painful."

The teacher looked at me and said, "Don't then. We can work out some alternative assignment or we can just start something entirely different." This statement erased some of the doubts from my mind. To this day, I will never know if he truly meant everything he said that day, and I will always have my doubts. However, he does once again have my respect because of one little line he said to the class. "I'm sorry if I hurt any of you. That was not my intent, and I was wrong."

I could now try to put Chad's death completely behind me. All the loose strings had been taken care of, and I suddenly felt an incredible sense of freedom that I had never felt before. I felt at ease with myself and the tragic events of the past week. I finally was able to think a little more intensely about the football game that evening.

Friday Night Lights

The heart-wrenching events of that week had not stopped the world from continuing on the way it always had. Momentarily, many lives paused and many others were permanently affected, like mine.

School let out on Friday. I rushed to my locker, and a group of my friends and I raced off to get some food. We had to arrive back at school in an hour because that was when the bus was leaving to go to the game. As we left to get a snack, I looked back at the school from my seat in the car. There were kids running out of it from all directions, and smoke continuously puffed out of it as it attempted to heat itself. The sight scared me. In the background was the hospital. It was hard to see over the school, and the lots between were divided with tall, chain-linked fences. The black road glared a reflection of the sunlight into my eyes. The grass was beginning to brown, most noticeably on the practice fields. The red clay bricks of the high school appeared to form a whole, but each looked to be standing as an individual.

We cruised down the road away from the school and arrived at a local pizza place to order some personal pan pizzas. We didn't want to eat too much, but we knew we had to eat because the next time we would get the chance would be around midnight. Over our food, we discussed many topics. Finally, the subject of playing in tonight's football game came up. I thought that I was the only one who didn't feel right about playing, but after I listened to those guys, I felt lucky. Many of them didn't even want to go to the game, much less play in it. One person kept saying that the game was meaningless because we were out of the conference lead and didn't have any chance short of a miracle of regaining it. But it was also meaningless in the overall picture of life. No one would remember this game in the winter, much less in ten years. It was a point I could not argue.

We finished eating and raced back to school. I walked into the locker room and got my stuff ready to put on the bus. On one side, where all the seniors had lockers, everything was beginning to get back to normal. They were all joking around, making noise, and having a good time getting their stuff together. The other side, where all of us juniors and a few sophomores were, looked as if it had seen a ghost. One might think it was pre-game concentration, and for some people it was; however, for others it was a much deeper feeling than concentration.

We boarded the bus, where I sat in a window seat. The bus's engine roared. I immediately fell asleep, the long week and very few hours of sleep beginning to catch up with me. When I awoke, I thought my dream had changed from one of pure darkness to one of a winter wonderland. The ground was covered with a white powdery snow. I rubbed my eyes and realized that this was no dream. It really had snowed while I was dreaming of darkness. I began to get nervous about tonight's game. It was going to be hard enough playing, but now I had to deal with snow. I was the center, and I had never snapped in the snow before. Supposedly, it made it much more difficult to do.

The bus arrived at the field, and we got ready to play. The locker rooms were about a quarter of a mile away from the field. That evening I suited up, putting on one of the wristbands I made in memory of Chad. It was my personal way of remembering that Chad would always be with me.

The team scattered and went down to the field, and I got lost somewhere in the middle. I was able to make out the brightly shining lights, reflecting off the snow. The Friday night lights appeared to create an illusion that everything was the way it was supposed to be on this particular evening. It was a very peaceful and beautiful sight.

Our first offensive set was nerve-racking. I had trouble snapping the ball the whole series, but somehow I managed it, and our team dominated the game. I don't remember much about the game, but we won 28-0 when many expected us to lose.

It all went back to what my friend said at lunch. "No one will remember this game in the winter, much less in ten years." He was right, but that didn't seem to matter. Even though I didn't play my best game, I felt good because it was important that I had played.

I was definitely on the road to recovery. The game itself was an important path on that road. I was able to release some of my anger and still perform adequately.

After the game, we rode back on the bus. The adrenaline was flowing so strongly through my blood that I couldn't sleep. I just sat and stared out the window at the white blanket covering the country roads and fields. It was beautiful.

We arrived back in town late. I remember it being eleven thirty or so, and I didn't leave the high school until about eleven forty. From there, I went with a group of the guys to McDonalds to get some food. We sat inside until about twelve thirty, even though they closed at midnight. It was fun because we could watch the workers get angrier and angrier as we took more and more time. Although we had been through so much that past week, we still hadn't learned all the lessons we should have about paying attention to other people's feelings. We had come so far and yet had such a long way to go.

We left, and I went home. I walked in the door and saw my parents, who had waited up for me. I told them that I thought I had a subpar game, but all they did was say how great and tremendous I played. At the time, I didn't want to listen to them because I thought they were lying to me. Now I look back, and I'm really glad they acted as they did. It helped me to maintain my good feeling and made me feel special once again, something that I had not had all week.

I had a couple slices of the pizza that they had ordered and discussed the game with them. It was now around one in the morning. They wanted to go to bed and told me that I should too because I needed the sleep. I didn't want to go to bed. I just wanted to relax. But after about ten minutes of relaxing and finding nothing on TV, I decided to go to bed. As soon as my head hit the pillow, I went out like a light to face a world of darkness.

Saturday

The nightmares avoided me that evening. It was nice just to dream of solid black, like staring into the sky at night, but without stars.

After waking up once earlier in the morning, I felt like I had just barely shut my eyes when I heard my dad asking me if I was ever going to wake up. I rolled my body over. It felt so heavy. The red numerals on the clock said one o'clock. I could not believe I slept that long.

After taking a shower and attempting to watch a college football game, I got up to find something else to do, but then I noticed a huge stack of newspapers sitting on the table. It dawned on me that I hadn't read any part of the paper all week, so I sat down and began reading the sports page from every day of the week. After that, I went back to read other sections when I noticed the local papers from the week. I opened them, the sports first. These were the papers talking about the homecoming game of a week earlier.

It had been one of the best games our team had played all season, and the paper recognized that. Then I started to read some of the other sections when I made a shocking discovery. There were very few, if any, articles about Chad. I searched every section of every paper, and I was only able to find two articles. How could a town just completely ignore something like this? Were they blind to what had happened?

I read those two articles because I wondered what the town felt about the events of the past week. It looked to me like they were not even affected by it, and those that came to the funeral had just come for the sake of appearance. The first of the two articles I read was an obituary. It stated when and where Chad had died and when and where he was born. I looked at the name of the city that he was born in, and it gave me a shiver. He was born in Forest Grove. That city name reminded me of the many times Chad and I had played in a forest near my house as kids. The obituary then listed all the various activities Chad had been involved in, where he had gone to school, and the surviving members of his family. Chad had been able to live such a wonderful life with his involvement in everything from soccer to skiing to flying and the love of the family he left behind. It now hit me how young Chad had truly been. It looked as though every member of his family had survived him. I also felt like the whole town should be listed as survivors.

The article went on to say that there had been a funeral service on Tuesday. I started to think about the funeral and seeing Chad's corpse lying there, and it was enough to give me a good scare. The pastor's name that had conducted the funeral was also listed. I remembered hearing and seeing him, but I could not remember anything that he had said at the funeral. Finally, the article mentioned where Chad would be buried and whom memorials could be given to in his name. I paused. One of my friends was being buried beneath the dirt. Distressed, I was just about ready to say that I'd had enough and I didn't want to read anymore. I planned to just read the second article I found and then go to sleep or something.

The title immediately caught my eye. "Expert urges family, friends to heed warnings of suicide." I thought, "Well, at least someone is trying to tell us that suicide is a problem." Other than this article, it seemed like the whole town had ignored a problem that had occurred before and would occur again. However, as I went on to read the article itself, I became upset. "If you believe his classmates, Chad had it all – friends, athletic skills, a sharp mind." What reason did the author have for not believing us? It was as if he were saying that we were all liars just because we were Chad's friends. I continued to read with a feeling of anger toward him, a stupid man with no understanding for my feelings or the feelings of my friends.

The article went on to say that the rest of the town had to watch for "copycat" suicides. People who felt so much guilt that they would do the same thing. I read that twice, thinking, "After what we've been through, none of us would ever do that." The story continued, remarking that one thousand people had attended the funeral. "That's all that was there? It felt like there were so many more people. That's only one-tenth of the town. That explains why there were so few articles. It was only a small portion of us that had been affected." It still didn't seem fair to me. A friend of mine dies, and there are only two measly articles, one of which can't even be classified as an article and the other filled with a lot of blame and finger-pointing. The second piece proceeded with the idea that there were relatively few parents there. "Bullshit!" I thought. There were plenty of parents there, and the ones that were not had to take someone home or were told not to come by their kids. The parental support was clearly there.

By now I was beginning to wonder what the whole point of the article was. It went on to say that there were many that thought that Chad didn't show any warning signs. Finally, the truth. I kept thinking, "It doesn't fit a normal suicide. I truly believe in my heart that this was a fluke thing due to the fact that he had a little alcohol in his blood." Then the article tore down this argument: "It was a snap judgment thing, in my opinion. All indications are that he thought this out. It just seemed like something was weighing heavy on his mind." This was a quote by the person who investigated the scene. How would he know if something was weighing on Chad's mind? He didn't know him. The author ended with this quote, "Just pass on to them that friends don't let friends drink too much."

It felt like the article was simply blaming Chad's friends and alcohol for what happened and that the whole town and all of Chad's friends were just a bunch of drunks who didn't care about one another. I was so angry. The article also gave signs to look for in a troubled teen. When I read all of these signs, I thought to myself, "You just defined a normal teenager's way of life. Where do the signs come in?" Not once did the article mention a place for people to go to or to call in search for help. It was as if the article was written to assess blame instead of acknowledging a problem, a disease.

Yes, a disease, that's what suicide is, and the article treated it like a common cold. I had seen enough. I put away the papers and decided to watch TV. I was just so angry that the town and the author could be so naive as to think that they could avoid this disease instead of acknowledging it and dealing with it. Then I saw a bookmark lying on the floor that said, "Delight thyself also in the Lord, and he shall give thee the desires of the heart. Psalm 37:4"

I don't know if I can.

Sunday

I woke up with the article engraved in my head. I realized that I could never totally push the memories of the past week out of my mind. I would only be able to put them aside. Last week I had missed church because it was homecoming and I had slept at a friend's house. Today was Sunday, and I felt a special need to attend. I don't know if it was because I hadn't been in church for a couple of weeks or because I was hoping to find answers for all my doubts.

What or who should I believe? Everyone seemed so sure of the fact that there was a God and there was a better life after this one. The unknown just made me nervous. I drove to church that day with one thought in my mind. "Please don't let the pastor talk about Chad. I don't want to hear any more." But something inside me did want to hear a sermon about Chad. That part of me wanted to hear the pastor's answers to the complicated questions that had been plaguing me.

I walked into church with a feeling of bewilderment. What am

I doing here? Have I been living a lie by coming to church all these years? Is there anyone who can help me? The events of the past week sent me on a journey where I questioned everything that I was ever taught. The bulletin had a picture of a sunrise that looked as fake and unrealistic as it really was. There was no sunrise that could compare with the one I had seen earlier that week. The bulletin's sunrise was trying to give me a false sense of security, one that I could not and would not accept.

The service continued along as usual, and I sat there as I did every Sunday struggling to stay awake so that I could hear the sermon. I was just about asleep when the sermon finally began.

This is what I had waited for the whole service, and I quickly woke myself up so that I could hear the pastor preach the message from the Lord. Amazingly, the focus of the sermon was totally off the anticipated deadly subject. Instead of hearing a sermon about Chad's death and the circumstances around it, I heard the pastor speak on "How to Relieve Stress." When I first heard this, I thought that he was somehow going to tie in the fact that there are good ways and bad ways to deal with stress, and the way Chad chose was a bad way, but the pastor didn't do this.

I sat there thinking to myself, "I came to church to find relief, to find answers to unanswerable problems, and to attempt to feel better in general, and the pastor gives a sermon on how to relieve stress. Doesn't he have any idea about the grief the youth of the congregation are going through? My friend died only seven days ago, and the church, as well as the whole town, had already forgotten his death. They had already done their part, and now it was time to forget that this incident ever occurred. The beliefs I had been questioning all week were now thrown out the window. My thoughts continued, "If there is a God, there is no way he would have allowed Chad to die, much less turn his back on the people like me that are left behind. I mean, it's the pastor's job to give the message of the Lord, and if there is nothing there about my friend, how loving can that God be?

I wanted to get up and leave church immediately. This service proved to me that I no longer belonged. I wasn't going to find any divine message that would spare me my pain or help me to deal with it. I was angry, shocked, and appalled that I worshiped a God who seemed to ignore my questions and problems. One Bible passage that the pastor presented in his sermon epitomized how I felt. "The word of God is living and active. Sharper than any double-edged sword, it penetrates even to dividing soul and spirit, joints and marrow; it judges the thoughts and attitudes of the heart. Nothing in all creation is hidden from God's sight. Everything is uncovered and laid bare before the eyes of Him to whom we must give account."

I pondered these words and thought, "I can feel the word of God plunging like a sword in the middle of my back. It feels as if each day he twists and grinds it further into my spine." Then I looked at the passage printed on the bulletin. If God can see everything, including inside my heart, why won't he give me the answers I need to move on and to feel like my normal self again? The pastor had just told us nothing could be hidden from God, but I wondered if the Lord had lost track of, misplaced, or discarded me. The pastor ended the service saying, "If you want to experience real relief from the pressures of life, then let God do His work in you."

I thought to myself, "I tried, and it didn't work, so now I'll find my own way." I had totally tuned out the rest of the sermon. Everything he said I twisted to fit my confused frame of mind. I heard what I wanted to hear, and yet these were the very same things

I didn't want to hear. It would be impossible to follow the advice of the passage from the bookmark. I would never be able to delight myself in the Lord and find the answers I needed. I had tried and felt betrayed, and I turned away.

A Second Chance

The next week was a blur. I looked around the school and saw that it was now completely back to its daily routines. I looked at my own life and saw that I too had fallen into the same patterns. There were very few individuals still openly stuck in the confusion and agony of the week before, and for the most part, I was no longer one of those individuals. I still had those dark thoughts circulating in my head, but I was able to separate them into a section of their own. Those feelings no longer destroyed my work in the classroom or my participation in sports outside of the classroom.

There were many who had not been able to make that step. Their grades fell, their participation in after-school sports suffered, and their popularity declined as they isolated themselves or were isolated from the rest of the school. It was hard to tell which really occurred. Despite observing all of this, I felt there was nothing I could say to those people because I was not one of their better friends, and I certainly did not feel I possessed the answers myself. I realize now that many of them just needed a friend to talk to in order to release their feelings and help them get through the tremendous torment that so many of us had already struggled through. My inability to befriend any of those kids who were entrenched in sorrow has always made me feel awful. At a time of such gut-wrenching suffering, individuals, friends or not, need to listen to each other and provide support, no matter how hard it is.

The week passed, and Sunday morning rolled around once again. My mom came into my room and found me exhausted, hugging my pillow. She told me I had to get up and go to church.

I thought to myself, "What's the point?" I used every excuse to avoid going.

None worked. I still don't understand why my mom badgered me so much to go to church that Sunday, but eventually I climbed out of bed and made my way there.

The only reason I tore my body away from the comfort of the blankets and pillows was because I felt a little guilt for being unable to help the people who were still struggling with the last couple of weeks.

Of course, by the time I got ready and arrived at the church, I was ten or fifteen minutes late. I couldn't help thinking that it was such a waste of time and there was no message for me or anyone my age there. I might as well be home watching TV or sleeping. As the service unfolded, I increasingly became more tired and less interested. My mom even knocked me lightly on the top of my head as I started to fall asleep.

The sermon rolled around, and I was ready for another message that meant nothing to me. It was as if I was in a foreign country, out of place, far removed from the comfort I was searching for. The pastor quoted a Bible passage. "All have sinned and fallen short of the glory of God, and are justified freely by His grace through the redemption that came by Christ Jesus." This phrase caught my attention.

I had been browsing through the bulletin and noticed that the sermon title was "The Hammer Blows." For some unknown reason, I suddenly felt awake and ready to listen. The pastor preached his sermon, and I got the impression that he was blaming the youth of the congregation for Chad's death. To me, it seemed to focus on the fact that the community thought of drinking as a solution instead of a problem. The sermon came off as directed toward our parents and other adults in the church and warned that they had to watch the drinking problem in our community. After hearing this, more anger built up in me. How could he totally forget to address us, the students, the ones most severely affected by the last two weeks? It felt as if he was once again blaming Chad's death on us, his friends.

I was crushed. I left church enraged by the thought that God had forgotten about me and my questioning of His existence. How could he let such a tragic event occur? How could I go to church hoping to find an answer and leave filled with new questions? Why does everyone think alcohol is such a problem? Everyone's been to a party once in a while where alcohol is served. I drove home in a daze, pondering everything.

I pulled into my driveway. The confusion war once again built in my mind. I watched the Packer game, but those haunting questions kept ringing through my brain the entire game. It was finally after the game that I sat down and wrote out a list of all the difficult questions I had, then tried to answer every question. Each question was answered differently than how I would answer them now. I knew every answer that I wrote was wrong, but they were answers that I could momentarily believe so that I could get on with my life.

Even today's answers may not be totally correct, but they allow me to have an answer for that particular moment of time until I can discover a better one, or maybe even the right one. The questions will never go away, but it helps to have some kind of answer that I can temporarily believe.

That evening, I had a conversation with my mom concerning the pastor's sermon, and she went on and on about how he did such a wonderful job. Confused, I looked at her and suddenly filled with rage. I wanted to lash out at her, but I just looked at her, nodded, and went and watched TV.

Recently, I obtained a copy of the pastor's sermon and discovered an entirely different meaning. It was as if on that Sunday, I paid attention to only one of the many things he said. I had concentrated on one sentence and lost the true meaning of the sermon. As I read and reread it, I found that the pastor had answers to many of my questions, but I was too narrow-minded to realize what he was saying. He pointed out that it took a tragedy to break down the barriers that are often put up by teenagers and acknowledged that the community was able to demonstrate such love and concern for Chad's family, and the principal, faculty, and staff of the high school were able to use their resources so quickly to confront a difficult situation and sensitively help in relieving the tension that grieving creates. He had in fact aimed the sermon at the youth of the congregation, and I had missed it because of one sentence.

The pastor explained that each individual has an abundance of importance in our world, no matter how meaningless or lonely they feel. The problems encountered by the youth today are huge, but never impossible to deal with. In order to properly deal with these problems, teenagers need the advice of adults who possess the experience and resources necessary to help. He also told us that, no matter how jokingly you intend your remarks to be, they can cut deeply. Every person has the power to hurt someone with their words. Words should be used to create confidence among one another, but it is not only words that speak. Our actions, hugs, looks, and little phrases like "hi" can speak volumes toward making someone feel better. A few phrases that the pastor spoke that day went a long way in helping me to recover.

> "The law, I found, was not the way
> To life and health, to joy and peace;
> I'd piled up debts I could not pay,
> From death there was no sure release.
> And then, when in the deepest throes
> Of gloom, I heard the hammer blows
> Constructing my salvation."[1]

This verse was something that held a lot of personal meaning, but for each person, there will be a new meaning discovered. It is something that one must ponder and take to their own heart. The pastor then began to wrap up his sermon with another quote.

> "The gift I had no right to claim,
> A life to compensate my loss,
> By grace from God the Father came:
> My Substitute upon my cross.

---

[1] "The Rescue We Were Waiting For" by Jaroslov Vajda, verse 3

My pardon there was read to me,
Beneath that God-forsaken tree—
And I am free forever!"[2]

The pastor, in essence, was saying that Christ, by his death, has made each of us priceless and important, and no matter how much despair or grief you feel, there is always someone there for you. It was this message that helped me release many of the doubts and confusion I had. The pastor's point that everyone is valued was not just a bunch of hollow words. Those words must be taken to heart to fully appreciate life.

---

[2] "The Rescue We Were Waiting For" by Jaroslov Vajda, verse 4

Life After Death

It has been close to a year now since Homecoming '91. The anniversary of Chad's suicide will arrive within two weeks. Yet I am more troubled by homecoming than the anniversary itself. Homecoming reminds me of all the good and bad memories of a year ago and the hardest lesson that I have ever learned in my life: death. The difficult questions and emotions that came with that lesson will always stay with me. My life will never be the same.

Since last year, I have grown as a person. I have been able to deal with those events and still live my life. I have been able to keep my strong emotions, troubling memories, and difficult questions alive, but in storage. However, in the past week, I have had memories slip through the cracks of my mind. I have been having trouble concentrating on my studies, my sports, my life, and I have sensed that some of my friends are having the same problems. This week of Homecoming '92 is bringing back so many memories, good and bad, of a year ago.

It is a tradition at our school to have theme day during the week of homecoming where we show school spirit by dressing up for a particular theme each day of the week. This year, the themes are almost exactly the same as last year. Thursday was cross-dress day, when all the guys dress as girls and the girls dress as guys. It is rare to find a guy that is daring enough to wear a skirt. When I see them, I think, "No one will ever be able to match Chad's outfit from last year." He came to school dressed in his mom's miniskirt, and his grin stretched from here to China. It is incredible how special that day is to me now. I'll never forget seeing guys walk up to Chad and say, "Hey, Chad. How's it going?" Then as they walked away, they'd add, "I saw him from a distance, and I thought he was some new girl that was really hot." Nothing this year can compare to that day.

This year just doesn't seem special. It feels like a total mistake to even repeat the theme of a year ago. It's so awkward not being able to see him. All week, I keep thinking that he's going to walk around the corner dressed as a hippie, or maybe a cowboy, or even as a girl in a miniskirt. I'm expecting him to show up and just tell me that he's been away on a long vacation. I know that it can't happen and that it won't happen, but I can't stop hoping that it will. Everyone else around the school looks so excited and so alive, and I know I should feel the same way, especially because it's my senior year, but somehow, I just cannot escape the memories from last year.

This is a strange kind of anniversary that I wish I would not have to experience. It makes me feel so weak when I really should be feeling my strongest. A ten-ton bag of bricks is weighing on my back. I want to get rid of it, but I can't. It's strapped on me, and I feel helpless to release the straps. It doesn't feel right for me to enjoy this week, these five days, without Chad.

At first, I thought I was the only person who had these feelings. Looking around, I would see all these people that were so happy and were working really hard to make this the best possible homecoming ever. It seemed as if I was the only one struggling to have a good time. However, after having a conversation with a friend of mine, this thinking all changed.

At the time Chad committed suicide, we were just acquaintances in the hall, but now she is quickly turning into one of my best friends. One night, we were studying AP European History at her house when I noticed the newspaper article about Chad hanging on a bulletin board on her wall. I asked her, pointing to the article, "Is it just me, or does this week seem too painful to have any fun?"

She said, "Yeah, I know what you mean. There's this feeling that nothing seems right."

"Exactly." I got up and walked over by the bulletin board. "Didn't this article piss you off when you read it?"

"Yeah, it made me really angry."

Instead of studying, we sat there and talked about our feelings and memories of Chad. This was really the first time I expressed to anyone during this year's homecoming week what I was feeling about Chad's suicide, and it was also when I discovered that she, along with many others, were still going through the same confusion that I was. This revelation helped me release some of the emotions that I had built up over the past year. We made a pact that later on in the week we would go to the annual Wednesday homecoming festivities together: the chili supper, the powder-puff football game, and the bonfire. Afterwards, we would visit Chad's grave. We figured that maybe this would help us deal with the many thoughts, feelings, and emotions that were circulating our minds.

The festivities of Wednesday night rolled around and went well for most of the school, but there were a few of us who could not seem to enjoy them. I was there physically, but mentally I was someplace distant, as if I was lost in another world. We arrived at the powder-puff game a little late due to the fact that I had a long practice that evening, but we caught the end of the game and watched the senior/freshman team beat the junior/sophomore team. I was so proud that our class won. Then we watched the bonfire and carried on conversations with many people.

I left with my friend as the bonfire was dying, and we drove silently to the graveyard. There was a little talk, but for the most part, all that could be heard was the radio.

I looked in the back seat of the car and felt a rush of relief when I saw that I remembered the flowers that I bought to put on Chad's grave. As I saw the flowers move back and forth on the seat, I began to get a funny feeling. It was an uncomfortable feeling that I knew I had in the past, but I could not place where.

Then it hit me. This feeling was the same as what I had experienced at Chad's funeral. I had forgotten how truly painful it was.

We arrived at the entrance to the graveyard and started to pull down the one-lane road that led to Chad's grave when I stopped the car just before the bridge and looked at the river. It seemed hidden in the darkness behind the cluster of trees that created its shoreline.

I was about ready to cross the river when I noticed a sign hanging on the bridge. "Graveyard closed at 8:30 p.m." I was scared. I felt like I couldn't breathe. Were we too late?

I quickly glanced at my friend and then at the clock in my car. The time was 8:28. The feeling of relief I felt was incredible. We continued driving down the path, crossed the bridge, and entered the cemetery. At the end of the one-lane road, we could see all the headstones, and the road now split in several different directions. I turned left, heading straight for the area where Chad had been buried. The night air was crisp and cool as we stepped out of the car, and darkness was a blanket that spread throughout the cemetery. It had been dark before we entered the graveyard, but somehow it seemed even darker once we passed its imaginary walls. That didn't matter though, because we knew exactly where to go. We walked right up to the grave. We had both been there so many times in the past, alone, that it didn't matter how dark it was. I walked over to Chad's grave and placed the roses that I bought on it. Suddenly, I had a flashback of the last time I had come here.

It had been a Sunday in late November. I had just attended church and was on my way home to watch the Packer game. For some unexplainable reason, I decided to stop and pay my respects. It was all on the spur of the moment. I got out of the car, walked up to the grave, and was appalled by what I saw. A soda can, empty and partially crushed, was lying on top of Chad's grave. I picked it up, looked at it, and then crushed it some more and threw it into a nearby garbage can. How could someone be so incredibly rude and disrespectful and litter on my friend's grave? I was filled with an uncontrollable rage and wanted to find this person so that I could inflict some damage. The hate created inside of me by one little piece of litter on Chad's grave made me suddenly realize how important graveyards can be. Graveyards are a place for loved ones to remember and respect family and friends that have passed and give those family and friends a place to deal with questions and concerns created from that death. They are a place for those that have been left behind to find healing and faith. This was something that I had not understood in the past, and it was unfortunate that I had to learn this way. My feelings and emotions waged a war inside of me again, a war that I eventually had to discard and ignore.

"Gavin. Gavin."

My friend was talking to me. She had just asked me a question, but I was in such a trance that I had not heard a word that she said. Then she asked me again. "Are you alright?" Suddenly I was hit with the weirdest feeling. Relief. It felt as if I had been carrying a burden all week, all year, and now it was gone.

I answered her, a smile cracking on my face, "Yeah, I'm fine." Now I understood that in the past, I had often come to the graveyard to hide from the problems, the reality of the world. I could now see that it was a place where I could begin to face these problems and this reality. The graveyard was a place that wasn't as grave as it looked or sounded, but instead was where someone could come to find inner peace. It was a place where people like my friend and I could unload all their feelings and emotions, similar in many ways to my discovery about the purpose of a funeral. I would never go to a graveyard again unless it was to search for such peace and happiness. The peace and happiness came from the fact that the burden I was holding on to for so long had finally been lifted.

I sat in that cemetery and talked to my friend for almost forty-five minutes, releasing my feelings and listening to her release her own. It quickly dawned on me that I had finally learned how to express my feelings.

Hopefully I will never lose that ability. The only way to deal with an event as tragic as suicide is to bring your feelings out into the open and listen to others express theirs. It is a long process, but it gets a little bit easier with every passing day. I remember listening to my friend as her breath steamed in the cold winter air. It was as if the air was talking to me. It was cold outside, but inside I was feeling warm once again. We sat there and talked about all the good times we had with Chad and how much we missed him.

Particularly, I remember talking to her about what Chad would think of all the changes that had occurred over the past year, including the difference in our friendship. We were good friends sitting next to his grave, helping each other deal with the pain of an awful anniversary, yet less than a year ago, we hadn't even known each other. This made me wonder about all the friendships that Chad missed by ending his life.

That evening, after my friend had gone back to the car, I felt satisfied with the way I had dealt with my emotions. I was ready to leave, but first I looked up at the sky. To my delight, millions of beautiful stars were shining. Each one seemed different, and yet they all seemed the same. It was the first time I had really bothered to look at the stars closely, and I was now able to see beauty in them that I had never seen before. This got me to wonder, "Where is Chad now?" It is a question that is so hard to answer and something I have still not found the answer to. It is a question I hope every year to be answered, but I am starting to suspect that it won't be answered until my time on earth has passed.

The following day in school, I was standing in the hallway that overlooked the commons area. I saw this kid with long blond hair, and I thought to myself, "Chad." I ran down to the commons to find him, but he was gone. He just vanished with no trace. Then about a week later, I was standing in the same spot when I saw the same blond hair. Racing down the steps, I was determined that I wouldn't miss him twice, and I didn't. Finding him in the commons, I walked right up to him and tapped him on the shoulder. He turned around, and to my shock and surprise, it wasn't Chad. My hope was crushed. I felt like an idiot as I apologized and explained that I thought he was someone else.

This horrid anniversary has brought back all the mixed-up emotions of a year ago, but this time they were easier to deal with. Maybe it's because I have been through the worst of it, that I've had almost a year to get ready for this anniversary, or maybe it's that I've learned that when I am scared, frightened, confused, angry, or lost, I must reach out. Every person needs to communicate his fears, griefs, and joys. Communication is the only way that we can stay whole and human. It is the only way to mend the emotional wounds that scar our souls.

The journey of contemplating life after death is a long one that will never end. With each anniversary of Chad's death, I will have to deal with completely new and different emotions as well as the resurfacing of the same old difficult ones. As time goes on, these feelings will hopefully get easier to deal with, but they are feelings that will always be with me. They will never go away, nor should they ever go away. As long as I continue to openly express them, they won't destroy me. These feelings will always be teaching me new, important lessons that may affect the way I feel toward life or toward my friends, but they will always be improving my life. This is all I can hope for as I travel down the unknown path that is my future.

Part III: Moving On

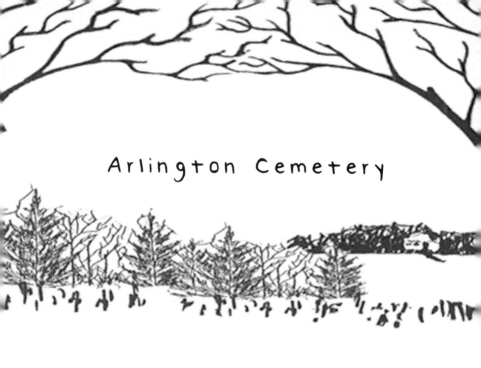

Arlington Cemetery

Homecoming came and went, as have so many things since the unfortunate death of Chad. That evening at the graveyard allowed me to shake the memories that had haunted me that week. They stopped slipping through the cracks in my head and were put back in storage where I could control them and they would help me, not hurt me.

That Friday, with the memory of Chad alive and stored away in my head, I went out and participated in our homecoming football game. We played in front of a crowd of over 5,000 people, and I went from the anxiety of not being able to control my feelings over the death of a friend to the nervousness and pressure of playing one of the most important football games of my senior year. The adrenaline coursed through my body as my teammates and I played our best and dropped our biggest rival. That game will always be special to me because, as I had before, I wore the wristband in remembrance of Chad and played my best jam inspired by his memory. We won 21-7, but that isn't what mattered. What mattered is that those of us who were most damaged by the memories of that week were able to put them behind us and begin to live our lives with a better understanding of where Chad's memory would fit into the rest of our lives.

Time passed, and slowly a new piece of my mind would heal. I began once again to feel invincible and that I would be able to forget the agony that had held me prisoner ever since Chad's death. However, that invincibility quickly shattered during the second semester of my senior year. I had a chance to visit the city of Washington, D.C., and, at the same time, escape the prison that I called school. It was the opportunity of a lifetime, and I snatched it up. I had the greatest time of my life.

That is, until I visited Arlington Cemetery.

It was a mild, rainy day in the middle of February when the group with which I was touring the city went to visit Arlington Cemetery. I got off the bus and was astounded at the beauty of this place on such a dismal day. A big green bush stood in front of me, and trees seemed to rise out of nowhere from behind the bush. Many of my newfound friends hurried near me to share my umbrella. We were the last bus, so we had to wait until the other three hundred kids got moving before we could go anywhere. We started walking like a herd of cattle, all bunched up. I was astonished by the scenery of the cemetery.

First, I looked behind me, and that single bush that I noticed now became one continual line of bushes that spanned as far as I could see. Only a few occasional breaks in the bushes made space for where statues were standing. I turned back around and saw a graveyard entrance to the right of me, and one to the left. The mammoth-looking walls, which had little devilish sculptures on them, and the huge black gates gave me an eerie feeling as the rain fell.

Looking straight ahead, I could see the street dead-end, and looming there was another incredibly monstrous wall. The middle part of it rose even higher than the ends, and it held the appearance of a heavenly temple. I followed the rest of the group as we slowly walked and gazed at the amazing scenery. It was breathtaking.

We entered the cemetery, and a queasy feeling emerged in the pit of my stomach. I thought that I was perhaps coming down with a cold. The feeling remained in my stomach as I marvelled at how many tombs there were. We walked up a path, and I looked over to my right, where I saw all the headstones lined up perfectly. They reminded me of a row of soldiers at attention. Each one ascended a little higher on a hill. That hill eventually took a drastic incline, and the headstones seemed to extend into the trees at the top of it.

I continued following the path and noticed a tan house with brown trim sitting on top of another hill at the highest point of the cemetery. It reminded me of those ancient Roman buildings with its tall majestic pillars, and it was as if this house overlooked the entire graveyard.

We climbed up toward the tomb of JFK, and my stomach trembled even more. I could not figure out why I was so nervous all of a sudden. I began to read some of the quotes surrounding Kennedy's grave, and I came across one that felt so real, like it was something out of my past. I was only able to capture fragments of the message in order to keep up with the group. "With a good conscience our only sure reward, with history the final judge of our deeds is go forth to lead the land we love and asking its and His help but knowing that here on earth God's must truly be our own."[3] This

---

[3] Actual quotation, from President Kennedy's Inaugural Address: "With a good conscience our only sure reward, with history the final judge of our deeds, let us go forth to lead the land we love, asking His blessing and His help, but knowing that here on earth God's work must truly be our own."

quote caught my attention, and I didn't understand why.

I arrived at the Tomb of the Unknown Soldier asking myself these questions: "Why is my stomach so queasy? Why did that quote hit me so hard? What did it mean?" I walked around in awe, admiring the beauty of the historic sight. It was amazing that it could be so beautiful on this day. There was no sunshine. It was raining intermittently and getting colder with each passing minute. I looked around the tomb when a soldier asked for the attention of our group. He said, "The following is a ceremony of the United States Army, and we would appreciate you showing your respect by placing your hand over your heart for the entire ceremony." The guards then proceeded to change the flowers on the Tomb of the Unknown Soldier.

This got me thinking about the different times I placed flowers on Chad's grave. I had not treated his grave like someone who was left in battle. I had never shown him the type of respect that the Tomb of the Unknown Soldier received. I would just place the flowers down, say a few words, and leave. This tomb had an entire ceremony that was treated with the utmost reverence. A solitary trumpet seemed to pierce my spine as I listened to each note that it played. Tears slowly came into my eyes, and I knew that I wasn't crying for the unknown soldier. I was crying because I had almost forgotten Chad by attempting to ignore my painful memories of him. I vowed to myself never to let this happen again.

With each note that the trumpet played, some of my many memories of Chad surfaced, both from when he was alive and when he was dead.

The face of reality was again knocking at my mind, and this time I decided to face it. I made a promise to myself that I would continue to visit Chad's grave in order to keep his memory alive, but controlled, in my head. Chad's memory will be with me for eternity. The one thing I knew is that I couldn't afford to forget what had happened and how it influenced me. This conclusion ended one path but sent me on a new one containing a new problem inspired by the quote from President Kennedy. The quote made me realize that I had to try and help others deal with the problem of suicide because I had already faced it. Otherwise the problem will continue to grow. My journey of life after death will never end. As a matter of fact, it has only just begun.

Newfound Friends

The path of painful confusion I had travelled on for so long had finally ended, and I discovered a new path that opened my eyes to the greater problems of suicide. I was able to see that suicide existed as a problem in every country, state, town, and city. It is an elusive disease that is as deadly as anything known to mankind, but also less publicized than most other diseases, as if it's been ignored for years, only temporarily faced by people when they have to.

I was at the airport waiting for my flight to leave from Washington, D.C. Earlier in the day, I had toured the city with some of my new friends who also had late flights. Most of them had already left by this point, but I still remained with one other person. She had brownish-black hair and blue eyes, and she wore a long black trench coat. A bright red shade of lipstick made her face look like it was bleeding. She was waiting for the same late flight that I was.

We were sick of the airport, and she wanted to have a cigarette, so we sat outside the airport in a little entryway right next to the street where all the taxis would drop off their passengers. It was somewhat enclosed, and we sat on a black windowsill so that she could smoke and I could read the sports page. Off to the right of us was an area where passengers could register their luggage. People were constantly registering and then walking right in front of us. I'll never forget seeing all those people walk by, staring at us as if they were thinking, "You damn kids." In the midst of all the commotion, we just watched them walk by. Everyone was always in a hurry, and no one would stop and strike up a conversation. In the half hour that we sat there, I didn't notice anyone stopping to admire the view.

Through the window, I noticed the airport shuttles frequently driving by, and off in the distance, the subway hurried to its destination. The sounds of these vehicles were drowned out by the roars of the engines of the planes that flew in and out of the airport. This constant commotion made the coming sunset all the more beautiful. The shuttles, the subway, and the planes all mixed naturally, as if they were all part of the sunset itself. The sunset was a peculiar reddish-orange tone, yet it allowed the powder-blue color of the sky to linger. This dangling blue reminded me of how I always appeared to be dangling in life. I didn't always know where I was heading or where I had come from. I just seemed to be there.

My attention was abruptly pulled away from the sunset by the voice of my companion, and we started a conversation.

During our chat, the topic of writing managed to surface. I found out that, like me, she also was interested in writing. I had a sample of some writing that I had been working on about Chad's death, and I let her read it. I needed an honest opinion from someone who was unrelated to my story.

She read three pages and then stopped.

I immediately thought, "Oh shit. It's not good."

She then asked me exactly what happened, so I told her the long and short of my story. That is when she told me a story that I will never forget.

I don't remember all of the details, but I do remember one sentence she said. "I once tried to kill myself."

Thousands of different thoughts raced through my head. "You did what? Why would you want to do something like that? Don't you know what kind of pain that causes, not only to yourself, but to everyone around you? That's one thing that is completely irreversible." However, I trapped all of these feelings in my head, only to stare at her and listen intently.

She went on to tell me how she saw the many people that could be affected by such an incident and that she was lucky enough to be unsuccessful in her attempt at suicide. She learned that she still had a life to live, and no problem was worth ending her life over. I looked at her and felt sorry for her. She had reached a state in her life where she had almost taken the wrong path, but was fortunate enough to stumble upon something better. A greater feeling came over me. Joy. Joy for the simple reason that she discovered the errors and potential repercussions of her thoughts and actions. She knew that suicide was not the answer and was something she should never have attempted, much less considered.

The impression she left on me has forever changed my life. It gave me a jump-start in the direction of a new path. I had always felt like no one could understand the way I felt, but I didn't see until now that this disease of suicide existed in full force in every part of the country.

Her story evoked my own memories of another tragic loss, one that happened on New Year's that year. Many of my friends had finally climbed over the hump of dealing with Chad's suicide and putting behind them the death of a friend when out of nowhere, another close friend of many of my friends committed suicide. I did not know him. I was fortunate enough not to have to experience the pain all over again. However, the impact of his awful death helped me see that something needed to be done to bring this disease out of the corners of the closet and into the open. Dealing with suicide is something that society has decided to avoid because they can't find the answers to the difficult questions that come with it. Society would rather take the easier road and run from it than face it. I found it incredible that in little more than a year after Chad's death, another teen from the same city would take his life. The new confusing emotions that another suicide had brought to the surface of my mind combined with the memories I had of the terrible past. Recollections of my own similar experience from a short time ago resurfaced. So many difficult questions plagued me again. "How could God, if there is one, do this to my friends twice in the time span of a little more than a year?" I still haven't found an answer to this question, and I wonder about it often. Chad's death almost destroyed my beliefs in God and the meaning of life. This most recent death forced me to examine my answers to my questions, and they were not sufficient.

Later that year, I wrote to a friend that I had met in Washington, D.C., and expressed my newfound doubts and grief. She gave me some good advice, something that one of her friends had told her. "Everyone goes through life living on a horizontal and vertical plane. When you are living horizontally, you are going through life just accepting things for what they seem to be. Life becomes vertical when you question and struggle with things. As you ask and discover your beliefs and morals, your life goes up and down vertically. If you never live vertically and always remain on a shallow horizontal plane, you will fall. It's the vertical times in your life that are hard but continue to give you support to keep you going."

This advice allowed me to understand that it was normal to have doubts about your beliefs even if you don't know what to do with them. Another path had been exposed for me to experience, one that would continue to make me face questions like, "Is there a God? Is there life after death? Is there a heaven and a hell?" The difficult answers that are held on that path are answers that I am in search of even today.

Remembrance of the Past

As all things eventually do, my trip and all my connections with it ended, and I was forced to resume my life. However, I was shocked by what I discovered. Very few people in school knew that I had been gone for a week. I felt unwanted, unneeded, and unnoticed. It was the strangest feeling of loneliness that I have ever experienced. What really shocked me was that there were even a couple of my teachers who hadn't realized that I had been gone. One teacher in particular had marked me in attendance for every day that I had been absent, and another teacher just thought I had skipped his class for a week.

This enraged me and made me feel like doing something drastic so that people would acknowledge my existence, but there was nothing that I could do. Eventually, as the day wore on, I was able to see that there was indeed a handful of people that did miss me, but for the most part, my absence had gone unnoticed. It was with this thought that I started to wonder how many people truly missed

Chad anymore. It was silly to think that everyone had forgotten him, but for some reason I had these doubts. Maybe these doubts arose from the fact that I had almost forgotten Chad a little less than a week ago or that my presence had been so easily forgotten.

It was all so depressing to me. I had all these weird thoughts that I didn't understand. "What would everyone think if I was gone for a longer period of time, not knowing if I would be back or not? Why does God allow people like me to feel so unpopular so easily? Why does it seem like no one remembers Chad?" If it hadn't been for those few people that noticed my absence, I might have been inclined to accept a life full of feelings of destitution and loneliness.

One of those few people who happened to notice my absence was a person who had been best friends with Chad and now slowly had developed into my best friend. He had been completely destroyed by Chad's death. Recently, he broke his arm, making it impossible for him to finish his sports season, but he said that the year before, he had used his sport to hide from Chad's death. He would take the pain of Chad's death with him to every event and punish his opponents by releasing pieces of that pent-up emotion on them. He had become unstoppable. Now, however, he had confronted and dealt with Chad's death and was ready to move on.

We sat down one day at his house and talked about the various good and bad times that we'd had with Chad, trying to piece together some answers that seemed reasonable to the both of us. We wanted to believe that Chad's death had been unintentional.

"Did you ever try to make yourself believe that Chad didn't kill himself, but that someone murdered him and set it up to look like a suicide?" he asked.

I looked at him. "Yeah, I had that thought a lot."

For an hour and a half, we sat there and talked about things concerning Chad. I'll never forget listening to him talk and seeing his face almost disappear into the blue wallpaper behind him. It was a weird feeling because I could hear what he said, but for some reason, some of the things he said would not register in my brain.

The main part of the conversation that I will always remember is that we had a chart filled with the memories of the people around the school and how they had dealt with Chad's death.

Even though it felt as if many had forgotten Chad, what they really had done was learn to put the incident behind them. They had found a way to go on living while still holding on to the many memories left to them by Chad. It was something that had to be done, and it took a long time for many people in our school to do.

I finally realized that nobody was forgetting Chad as I so conveniently thought, because that was impossible. Everyone in the school had done a good job of dealing with his suicide, something none of them should have had to do, and now they were moving down their paths with the memories of him following along.

That friend and I decided to go sledding that weekend. We drove through a foggy haze as we went through town, arrived at the hill, and climbed to the top of it. When we arrived at the tip of the sky, the view was breathtaking. The entire town glowed in its artificial light, and I felt as if I was in another world. I had never before seen beauty in this way.

I was above the fog and able to taste the cool, crisp air that reminded me of how beautiful life can be. On this night, all my feelings and emotions came together in my head, and I was able to understand that I had a lot of life ahead of me and a lot of memories of Chad from the past to cherish. This reminded me of what that compassionate teacher had told me in those first days after Chad's death. "You have to live your life as you always have, holding on to all the memories of Chad." At the time I had heard those words, the idea had sounded so ludicrous, but now I knew that it was the best possible advice that anyone could ever give me.

I suspect I will always have mixed feelings about Chad for the rest of my life. Whenever I think of him now, a smile will come to my face because of the memories I shared with him, but tears will accompany that smile because of the hurt he caused me and the helpless rage I continue to feel . . .

A Vision of Life

Time continues on. As I travel down the road of life, I have been constantly pointed in the direction of new paths. There were times that I would walk for weeks, unable to find a new path, while other times I would uncover a new road every day of the week. Each path I traveled on opened my mind to new questions, while many of them closed the book on others that were circulating in my head. I was able to heal a little more with each new path I found. Another year passed, yet I still hadn't found the answers to the questions, "Is there a God? Is there life after death? Is there a heaven and a hell?"

I was in a frantic pace running throughout my house. I was on track to be ten minutes late for school. In the past, this wouldn't have been a problem, but this year, I had a teacher who would not accept any kind of excuse for tardiness. His rule was that if you were late, even by a second, you would get a fifteen-minute detention. I missed the freedom I had last year when I could come to school any time I wanted.

I continued to race through the house. "Where are my shoes? Where are my keys? What did I do with my wallet?" Calmly, my mom responded, "They're over by the picture window." I turned and looked toward the twenty-foot picture window that stood about fifteen yards in front of me. Scattered on the floor around the dining room table were my shoes, keys, and wallet. I quickly walked to the window, following the brown carpet across the room, then down a step. The first light of the morning was beginning to shine through the window, then, after an instant, it disappeared behind the clouds. It was a fall morning. The trees were gently swaying back and forth, and the leaves quietly rustled as they were swept across the hill in the yard. The waves from the lake boasted their strength as they crushed against the rocks on the shoreline then flowed back out into the lake.

As I gazed upon that mystifying lake, it looked so peaceful and yet so very violent. My eyes wandered to the sky. The sun no longer sparkled off the soothing, vicious waves of the lake. The sky seemed so awkward. It was beautiful along the horizon as it displayed magnificent red and orange colors, but as my eyes shifted, I noticed that the sky, normally a shade of light blue, became dark. It was like the darkness of the sky blocked all the answers I so desperately wanted and needed. It also drew me back into my memories, the good and the bad. It was as if it pulled me into a trance that I will always fight to avoid. My world vaporized, and I found myself fighting to escape an entire world that lay ahead.

VROOM! VROOM! VROOM!

The vivid sounds of the roaring bus engine were drowned out by the cries and shouting of the children on it. The noises are so powerful and often unheard by adults. The bus raced down the highway as I traveled home from school that day. Every one of the kids on that bus acted with a new exuberance and excitement for their weekend plans. Today was Friday. We were released from the doors of the prison that our parents called school to party in the freedom of a weekend. However, at the age of seven, my idea of partying was extremely different from what it would be ten years later.

I had invited one of my friends to stay over at my house. He was a young boy with blond hair, long enough to be put into a ponytail. He was similar to me in size, and we were both younger than we looked. Instead of calling him by his first name, I yelled "Marsh!" He was sitting only a couple of feet away on the other side of the bus, but I had to yell at him because the noise level made it seem like he was several miles into the distance. Again the engine roared as if it were struggling to carry all of us to the safety of our homes.

VROOM! VROOM! VROOM!

I looked around the bus at all the kids sitting on the hard, green, vinyl seats. The bus was getting closer to my stop, only a couple of miles away, and I decided to pass the time by counting the seats on the bus. There were twenty-six seats, thirteen on each side. Marsh was sitting on the thirteenth seat on the right, while I was sitting on the thirteenth seat on the left. It was time for both of us to get off the bus.

The red stop sign popped up, and the doors opened. I got up and walked down the aisle. Meanwhile, Marsh jumped out the emergency exit.

We were running full steam trying to beat each other to the house. Marsh was about a step ahead of me as we felt the wind race through our hair. He beat me to the door, but he was locked out. I knew that the door was locked, and I didn't have a key, so I raced around the house and found the open door into the basement. I entered the house and let Marsh in. I had won the race!

We changed clothes, and now it was time to put our weekend plans into action. Marsh and I both wanted to walk down to the lake in our neighborhood, which was something that was very exciting to us. It was the freedom that we wanted, that we needed.

Leaving my house, we followed the road as it dropped down and slowly rose again. We traced its path for a quarter of a mile, then the road took a turn to the left. Instead of following the turn, Marsh and I gazed across the cornfield that was straight ahead. There was a sign that said, "No Trespassing. Violators will be prosecuted."

We stood on the outskirts of the field, pondering whether it was worth the risk to keep going. The field was beautiful. The stalks were all yellow and dead, but they somehow were able to stand up as if they were hiding something. I picked up some of the dark black soil in my hand. It was so smooth. There didn't seem to be any rocks, but then Marsh scooped up a handful a little deeper and felt nothing but rock. We both were excited to explore such a mystifying place. It was so much more exciting than anything around our houses.

I began to wander into the field, trampling over cornstalks and making a path of my own. About seven rows in, I looked back at Marsh. He seemed unsure about entering the field, so I told him not to worry about the stalks, that they were meant to be knocked down. He disagreed and found a path about thirteen yards to the right. I had traveled down that path before, and I knew that it wasn't any fun. You couldn't destroy anything, and someone could easily see you. We continued through the cornfield on different paths, each wondering what challenges their path held for them. I got so caught up in my adventure that I forgot that Marsh was even traveling with me until we met up at the end of the field.

I was glad to see him, but somehow he appeared different to me, as though things had changed between us. It was hard to pinpoint, but there was something unusual and awkward about him. I was different too, but I didn't know why. I just knew that I was different. It was probably because Marsh took the easier route, and I knew that my path was a longer and more difficult one. However, after traveling it, I felt rejuvenated.

I finally figured out what was different about Marsh. He looked run-down and exhausted, as if he went someplace that he wasn't meant to travel. We briefly exchanged a look, and then we left the field.

There were a few weeds that we were now standing in as we gaped at what was in store for us next. It was a forest. The forest was monstrous, but it also seemed like something that we could conquer. I felt it calling my name, challenging me to explore the beauty and mystery it held. The trees hidden in that forest had leaves painted with beautiful fall colors: red, orange, green, brown, and purple. Each leaf helped the forest sparkle and enhanced its beauty. As we stood there, a red fox ran right in front of us and then went into an area where someone had already trampled a path.

Marsh's eyes immediately lit up as they often had in the past. He looked like the Marsh that had explored the cornfield with me. "Let's follow the fox," he said.

I thought to myself, "No, let's go through the woods and cut him off," but then said, "You go ahead. I want to explore the forest a little more." Marsh went running down the path after the red fox while I gathered my courage to travel into the forest. I stepped in and crushed a twig, cracking it in half so it could never be reassembled. I continued to explore more and more of the forest, choosing which way to go and what to follow. It was a great, exciting journey, one that showed me a lot about myself and the world around me.

Finally, I made it to the end of the forest. I was at the top of a hill and felt like I could see forever. At the bottom of the hill, what looked to be a swamp led to a beautiful blue lake. It was hard to believe something so ugly could lead to something so stunning. I glanced back at the forest and began to wonder where Marsh had gone.

I turned back around and looked at the lake. Its beauty was overwhelming. It felt like all life's answers were right beneath its surface.

Then I noticed Marsh climbing into a boat. I ran down the hill, yelling at him, "Wait up!" but he didn't seem to hear me. Then I tripped over a rock and tumbled down the hill until I landed at the swamp. I got up and ran along the edge of the swamp until I reached an area where the lake and the shore came together. I kept yelling, "Wait, Marsh, wait! Don't leave me! I want to go out on the lake too!"

He yelled back, "Go home. I'm going to a better place. You'll find your way there, but now isn't the time." I stopped to think for a moment, then yelled, "Why?" But it was too late. Marsh had already disappeared into a misty haze about halfway across the lake. I stood still, frozen in place by our long-distance conversation.

I picked up a rock and played with it in my hands, trying to imagine where Marsh had floated off to. The lake looked like a glass window. I chucked the rock at the lake as far as I possibly could, and it barely made a ripple.

As I turned around to start my journey home, I noticed a bunch of cornstalks lying on the shoreline. These stalks seemed similar to the ones I had trampled over in the field, but when I looked closer at them, I noticed big black and red bugs crawling all over the stems. I wondered if Marsh actually took the path I thought he had. I turned toward the lake to see if I could catch one final glimpse of him.

His journey would make that impossible. Marsh was gone, but a big green fish jumped, creating a gentle ripple in that blue glass-like lake. I finally noticed that the swamp wasn't a swamp after all, but a marsh.

I had seen enough, more than I wanted to see, and decided to start my journey home. I traveled back up the hill in an attempt to reach the forest, but the hill seemed steeper now that I was alone. It was a hike to make it to the top, and when I got there, I needed to rest before entering the forest. The massive forest that had been so beautiful before now looked dark and terrifying. The trees were still calling my name, but the rustle of the leaves was now hauntingly different. The warmth of their brilliant colors had turned cold, and their lifelike rustle had been silenced, creating an eerie feeling. Many of the leaves had fallen to the ground and had been buried in the dirt. Others were holding on to the branches for dear life. The trees also appeared to be different, like redwoods instead of the pine and oak trees that they had been on the way in. I wandered into the forest very tentatively. It was a place that had lost its beauty, and I wanted to avoid it and find a new route home. However, for some unknown reason, part of me still needed to explore it more.

With each step I took, I became even more trapped by the presence and the shadows of the trees. Fear consumed me. I didn't know where I was or how I would get home. Every time I decided to go a new direction, it didn't work out. I decided to stop and mark a tree to find out whether or not I was walking in circles. A few hours later, I found the same tree with the same mark, blood from my cut finger. I had no other option than to go the completely opposite direction. I had avoided going this way because it seemed forbidden to me, and I didn't think I would be capable of handling the deeper struggles of the woods.

Wandering aimlessly for what felt like miles, I found a beautiful little clearing that had a small creek of flowing water with rocks scattered neatly throughout it. A bridge crossed over a creek. It was nothing fancy, but it looked as though it would do the job. I crossed the river and re-entered the forest. I knew exactly where I was and understood the direction I had to go to get home.

I journeyed out of the forest with a feeling of pride. I had found more than one path to explore, and I knew that there were endless paths that I had not yet traveled. I looked at the cornfield. Some of the dead stalks were now green and full of life, and the dried, dead, yellow stalks blended in, small and meaningless. I had found my way through the forest and knew that the path through the cornfield would be easy in comparison. Excited, I felt like I had new energy, so I raced through the field, running over anything and everything that got in the way.

I burst out of the field feeling better about myself, and I felt a need to explore the world around me. I wanted to go home, but it just didn't seem like the right time, so I decided to continue down the path that Marsh and I had stopped traveling on before. That path, the road, seemed to go on endlessly into the distance. It appeared perfectly flat, but when I looked closer, I noticed that the road eventually ended, and I would be forced to go right or left. Another cornfield stood just beyond the end of the road, and trees that lined the right-hand side seemed to point to that cornfield. I began walking down the road when I stopped to look at the horizon. There was a strip of blue across the top of the sky, but it was drowned out by the wonderful magnificence of the red and orange sky. This beauty was calling my name.

Gavin, Gavin, Gavin. Stop staring at the sky, otherwise you'll be late for school. Hurry up, it's where you should be.

"I'll be right there."

I looked out the window at the sky again and felt relieved. Its beauty was something I'll never forget.

"The heritage of the past is the seed that brings forth the harvest of the future."

Afterword

Suicide is a problem that is plaguing our nation. This is the general belief of many in the United States and around the world. However, in reality, suicide is a disease that is slowly destroying the future of our country. In 2016, around 45,000 died from suicide. Suicide is the second leading cause of death for people age 10 to 34 and the fourth leading cause of death for people age 35 to 54. Experts believe that horrendous statistics such as these are only the tip of the iceberg, and if all cases of suicide and attempted suicide were reported, the above figures would triple or quadruple.

There are many individuals who believe that unless this disease is examined and studied, it will continue to explode and harm its victims. With each suicide, there are people left behind filled with emotional turmoil and pain. The victim's family, friends, and community become engulfed in a sea of agony that they don't know how to handle and shouldn't even have to face. The hard and honest fact is that the person that commits the act is the innocent victim.

They don't understand what they're doing because they are suffering from depression. Depression is a deeper kind of suffering than most of us could ever imagine. Most people think that depression refers to a mood that all of us experience at one time or another in response to disappointments, frustrations, and the overwhelming grief that fills our lives. In suicide victims, depression is an endless feeling of hopelessness and futility that lasts weeks and, in some cases, years. It can begin with something minor but then can escalate into something that uncontrollable. Most stages of depression generally begin with a feeling of failure toward family, friends, or the individual himself. Then the individual will begin to isolate himself from the rest of society.

Generally speaking, depression can be linked to a wide range of causes. An individual may feel that he has become a failure because he has received lousy grades in school or he doesn't have any friends, to name a couple examples. Instead of attempting to right the wrong, the individual will become entrenched in deeper states of depression. He may increasingly become truant from school and his job. He may attempt to hide from his problems and his feelings of futility by getting into drugs and alcohol. He will turn to destructive behavior, rebelliousness, and take on a general attitude of disobedience. This disobedience will allow the individual to detach himself from support systems such as family, friends, and school. He will isolate himself, dwelling on his feelings of inferiority and futility by escaping into a world of loneliness where he is left to deal with his guilt and solitude. He will alienate himself from the rest of the world. Depression is a disease that can eventually lead to a distortion of reality as the individual destroys his mind and body.

Depression is a cause of many suicides, but not the only one.

Other suicides are caused by pressures applied from parents, society, and academics. Kids become hung up on the fact that they have to excel and impress everyone they see, whether it's a boss, teacher, their friends, or their parents. It's when they are no longer able to get the attention of these people that they obtain a low sense of self-esteem and a feeling of helplessness. They focus on things ranging from peer pressure, unbearable pain, poor health, academic troubles, and the pressure placed upon them to succeed in their everyday world. To many young adults, the disparity between expectation and accomplishment is the final devastating factor. They feel that if they aren't making strides in determining their future, their life has become hopeless and, therefore, no longer worth living. What they don't understand is that it is normal to hit all these bumps in their lives. In fact, there will be many times when they run into a wall that will seem insurmountable. What they must do is survive the hurdles because those are what add meaning and love to their lives.

It is important for friends to help each other through these hard times. We must offer a bridge between the isolation the suicidal person feels and the help they need to survive. It is important to always be aware of what your friends are saying and the way they are acting and to listen to them and provide them with support, even on the most trivial of matters. Don't discard their problems as meaningless, but rather listen to what they say, offer a solution, be honest, and share your feelings about it. Sometimes, you may have to tell them something that they don't want to hear, but in the long run, it will be better for the both of you. Help them understand that with each problem, there are many ways to deal with them, and suicide is not one of them.

Offer solutions to the victim. Explain to him that we all have problems and that the only way we can solve them is to seek help. Don't ever count on the fact that the problem will just go away, because the longer it isn't dealt with, the more it will linger, and the worse it will become. If you are unsure of how to handle a situation, get help from another friend or an adult. Cooperate with what the victim has to say so that he will be more willing to seek the help of others. Suicide must be dealt with out in the open instead of being pushed into the closet as society has for so many years. The longer that everyone continues to ignore it, the already large percentage of deaths will become larger and larger. Society is more comfortable acting as if this disease doesn't exist, and this has only helped expand the problem.

For years, society has said, "I don't care if you kill yourself. I don't think you should do it, but I'm not going to stop you. It's kind of a dumb thing to do, but if you insist on doing it, it's not going to affect me one way or another." Some people will occasionally say, "That's too bad" and allow it to momentarily touch their thoughts. But after a few seconds, society will once again push the situation behind closed doors or into a corner somewhere because they don't realize how dangerous suicide can be. There will be a few articles that will analyze it, and your friends will mourn. But the mourning will eventually end, and you will become another fading memory.

This attitude must be replaced with a new attitude and philosophy. It is important for the future that we educate our youth today about the myths and the facts of suicide. In 2016, 9.8 million people in the United States thought about committing suicide, with 1.3 million people actually attempting it. Suicide is not some genetic defect that runs in families. It is a disease that affects individuals in different ways. Very few of the people who become statistics are mentally insane. Many of them are not in their ordinary frame of mind, but this is very different from insanity.

Friends can help bring an individual out of this suicidal state of mind by simply talking about the issue. Such a discussion will help relieve the intense pressures created by their emotional suffering. Victims of suicide rarely want to die. Most are just seeking attention or reaching out and asking for help. If a friend confides in you, the worst thing you can do is tell them that suicide is a dumb thing. It is important to acknowledge their pain and confusion, build up their confidence, and make them feel special. This friend is just a person that needs to know how much they matter and how deeply they are needed.

Don't ever abandon someone who is showing signs of being suicidal. Help him through the difficult period by encouraging him to talk to you, and then to a teacher, counselor, pastor, or family member. It is of the utmost importance to show concern and support. If the individual refuses to go to an adult for help, it is your duty to alert the attention of someone more knowledgeable so that you can help your friend. Be prepared to seek help when the friend shows warning signs such as giving away all his valuables, noticeable changes in eating or sleeping patterns, unexplained violence, withdrawing from friends and family, running away, persisting boredom, decline in schoolwork and school-related activities, a radical personality change bringing forth a sudden obsession with death, or jokingly discussing suicide or bringing it up in casual conversation. It is important to be loyal to your friend, but you must realize that this is too big a burden to keep secret. Keep your loyalty by allowing your friend to express how he is feeling to you.

Monitor your friend on his use of drugs or alcohol. Your friend my decide to overindulge in substances so that it looks like just another irresponsible death when, in reality, it was a suicide. Drugs and alcohol act as depressants and often increase the feelings of depression and impulsiveness. It is important to make sure that someone is always with your friend because the worst thing to do is to leave someone alone that is pondering suicide. Be suspicious if your friend attempts to get rid of you. Suicides are usually planned out and are very rarely impulsive acts.

The signs of suicide can often be minute, and that is why everyone must be educated about them so that even the slightest signal can be caught. If you are contemplating suicide, get help. You are not alone. There are many organizations that help people like you. Talking to your friends, respected adults, or those that you are closest to is something that needs to be done. The pain that suicide creates is something that no one will ever get over or forget. Their life will always lack something. You!

If you are embarrassed to share your feelings, you shouldn't be. You have so many reasons to live, even if you don't think so. There have been many people who have felt the same as you and have turned their lives around into something special. It is important to seek out these people and see what they have become. Listen to the lyrics of some of the songs that talk about it. Billy Joel tells of his experience in "You're Only Human (Second Wind)," while John Lennon and Paul McCartney discuss the disease in "Yesterday."

Time can drag on when you are young and entrenched in a world of problems. You have so much time to think. As you think, consider all the people that love you, and those that consider you a friend, and those that depend on you. You can't give up on life just because it holds so much unknown. No matter what type of pain is burning in your soul, it will eventually heal. If you commit suicide, you only destroy that chance to heal.

It is a difficult story to tell but one that must be told so that young people understand the grief involved and the many people they impact with their act. For every deadly suicide committed, a thousand lives could be affected. Those thousands of lives will affect thousands more, and so on. Once the act is committed, you will damage thousands of lives, and you will be gone forever. Suicide does not just destroy you, but it destroys everyone around you. If you have a friend that commits suicide, don't follow his example. Stop and take a look at the world, at the anguish that he caused you and your friends and think to yourself, "Would I want to do this to anyone?"

In order to deal with a suicide, you must deal with the event itself. The more the event is denied, the harder it gets to eventually deal with. Don't be afraid to discuss your feelings with a psychologist. You aren't crazy, you're just looking for answers. Answers can also be provided by your pastors, parents, teachers, and counselors. The support that these people can provide will go a long way in keeping you mentally strong and healthy.

It is also important to realize your emotions. Stuffing your feelings inside will do nothing for you except create more inner agony. Don't be afraid to cry. It isn't a sign of weakness, but rather a sign of pain. It is also very important to attend the funeral, no matter how impossible it feels. It is your chance to say goodbye. It will be hard, but it is something that you will forever be thankful you did. Attending your friend's funeral will also allow you to move on in your own life and regain control of your life. It is also important for schools to realize that this is not a problem that will just go away. They must educate teenagers and teachers so that they can heal. Don't force them to heal in a predetermined time period. Guide them to psychologists, but don't force one down their throat.

For many people across the United States, each suicide is just another statistic. They are dead wrong. Each number represents so much more. This is my story.

Suicide is a growing epidemic past the stage of simply plaguing our society or only destroying part of it. It is now destroying the future of tomorrow by destroying our youth. With each individual that we lose to suicide, we could be losing the next president, the next great inventor, the next amazing mom or dad, or the next best friend.

Please don't discard suicide as just another teenage problem, because it isn't. It is a disease that must be dealt with through open doors. It should never be locked away in a corner with the hope that it cannot harm us. It already has.

In the end, I know that people affected by suicide can move on and be successful. The result of this horrible problem in our society is that people learn about life and death. People learn about mourning. People learn about moving on. A Marshland of His Own was my attempt to move on from a suicide of a friend, and as I reworked and re-read this book in 2018, I found how truly important it is to be aware of the statistics and the problem. I want to educate people about the feelings of those left behind from suicide. Hopefully this book will help someone decide not to commit such an act. Hopefully this book will help someone see that they are not the only one to ever have to face such a horrible situation. Hopefully this book will become a source of healing and a blueprint for many to move forward. If you are struggling with the thought of suicide or with dealing with a suicide, please realize that there is help out there and use this book to see that you are not alone. No matter who you are, you are loved, and you have a future. Hold on to that even in your darkest and deepest moments.

Acknowledgments

The message that has been delivered in this book is necessary for the survival of our future. It would not have been possible for me to create without the help of some very intelligent people.

I would like to thank my mom, Suzanne Zastrow, for the numerous hours she spent photocopying my original story. Without those photocopies, I would have been unable to obtain the help of anyone else. Looking back, the conversations and love she showed me when she did not understand me is superhuman in nature, and I thank her for always knowing the right thing to say even though she didn't know the right thing to say. Mom, you have always been there for me, and I feel so blessed to have had your influence on my life.

My dad, David Zastrow, along with my mom, provided me with much meaningful insight as to where I could improve my story. I would also like to thank them for providing me with the materials to produce my message. They pushed me to feel good about my writing. When I was ready to quit, they were always there to support me. In future tragedies I encountered in my life, as in this one, my dad always seemed to know just the right thing to say to me to keep me moving forward in life instead of getting permanently left behind. I would also like to thank my parents for their never-ending love and support. Every year, they continue to share their knowledge and wisdom with me and make me a better person. Words cannot express the love and gratitude I have for all they have done for me in my life and all they continue to do. Their wisdom in this book was only built upon with future events in my life that were more difficult. Their knowledge got me through those situations as well, and I will be forever aware that I would not be the person I am today if it wasn't for their influence and love.

I would like to thank Mary Jo Newburg, a teacher at my high school, who spent a great amount of time helping me correct my grammar and make the story more universal. I have always appreciated the time and effort she put in to allow me to deliver my message. It was also her encouragement that made me continue. Even when I produced a meager chapter, she showed me a way to improve it and then encouraged me to do better. As I look back at the whole process of creating this story, I now realize that this teacher may be the best teacher I ever had, even though I never sat in her class. Even upon publishing this book, she has asked me questions that have inspired me to dig deeper and reflect in a way that most people can't get me to do.

Lyn Reed is another person who made the production of this book possible. She spent much of her free time, which was very little, editing a copy. Many of the changes that I made were due to her influence. She allowed me to see a parent's reaction other than my mom and dad. I owe her a great deal because she helped me to send my message and make it clear for all people to read.

I would also like to thank Cori Freudenburg. She was a friend who provided me with a teenager's opinion. We were very good friends even though we lived in different cities. It was her friendship that helped me to continue the book when I felt I didn't want to anymore. She also helped me with my struggle over religion. She provided me with advice through letters, and when I really needed a friend, I knew she was always there for me. She gave me an opinion of someone who knows none of the "characters" or history of the story. As I look back, she was definitely a guardian angel watching over me when I needed support (I firmly believe that today).

My cousin, Jenni Zastrow, was instrumental in the advancement of this book. It originally started as a short story. I allowed her to read it, and she said, "This is a good short story, but you need more. In order to make it as good as it deserves to be, you have to relive the painful memories of that week. You have to include the reader instead of isolating him from your feelings." It was with this advice that I was able to see how to turn a weak ten-page draft into the strong, powerful story that it is.

I would also like to thank Joe Krause for his original artwork. I had a vision of what I wanted the cover of this book to look like, but had no artistic ability whatsoever. Joe lived near my house, so I walked him down to the property that I wanted as a cover of this book and said, "Can you draw that?" He did, and it made a perfect template to be cleaned up for the publishing of this book. That location as drawn no longer exists, as houses have been built in its place; however, I will never forget what that peaceful place looked like at that moment in my life because of the image drawn by Joe. Thanks Joe!

Finally, I would like to thank all the good people at Orange Hat for helping me make this book a reality. It has a truly powerful message that needs to be shared, and thanks to your process of publishing and editing, that message will now be available for anyone who needs it.

GAVIN ZASTROW, known to many as Z, is a teacher at Stone Bank School in Stone Bank, Wisconsin, where he has worked for many years. He received his Bachelor's in Education from Miami University in Ohio and his Master's in Administrative Education from the University of Wisconsin-Milwaukee. He also obtained his Reading 316 and 317 licenses from the University of Wisconsin-Madison. Gavin has lived in Oconomowoc, Wisconsin, for most of his life, and enjoys reading, sports, spending time on Okauchee Lake, and being with his family.

CPSIA information can be obtained
at www.ICGtesting.com
Printed in the USA
FFHW021353190119
50146335-55047FF